ONE NIGHT TWO LIARS

Brian G Burns

BB.
BOOKS

Cover picture copyright: kallejipp/Photocase.com

Cover design, typesetting and unfailingly generous support:

Rita Wüthrich

Thanks also to Robert Saunders, John Clarkson and Kate Flagg

For my parents, who didn't get to see this book.
I don't flatter myself it would have been to their
liking, but they would have been pleased all the same.
More than that, you cannot ask.

Contents

A blow to the head

He turned the corner into Camden Passage and stopped to catch his breath. In the swelling humidity, he rested his left hand on a shop windowpane. Pink sweat trickled into his right eye. His head hurt badly.

Through the glass, he could make out a woman behind a counter at the back, wrapping bowls in newspaper. A man walked down a flight of stairs behind her and out through the back door. She stopped what she was doing and followed him out.

He squinted and a large trunk shoved against a fireplace tuned into view.

That'll do. I'll get it all in there.

Inside, it was cool. Out back, the man and woman were talking, her voice blunt, his clipped, and nothing between them clear.

The trunk was guarded either end by Chinese screens, their latticework chipped and faded. A bone-handled hunting knife on the mantelpiece caught his eye. In the fireplace, in a murky tank on a rickety wooden trolley, two fish chased each other's tails. On the wall above hung the head and gutted pelt of a fox, its mouth snapped open in fixed surprise.

In the mirror, a face more brutish than handsome surprised him. His fair hair had darkened, and hung greasy and limp. Eyes once bright were drilled deep into blue-black shadows. He could hardly see the bloodshot for the pink.

How big was that last one? Very. How many big ones? Too many.

He draped his jacket over his left forearm to hide the blood on his shirt, and knelt to examine the trunk. It was splintered in places, and damp on one side, but it would do.

He heard a noise at the back step and stood up, his right hand on the mantelpiece for support. Through sparks of light he saw the woman standing there, a silhouette, soft, small, round and silver.

'Sorry,' she said, 'I didn't hear anyone come in.'

'That's OK.'

'Interested in the trunk?'

'Yes.'

She turned her head and called out back, 'Jack, you have a customer. Likes the look of the big trunk.' She turned back to him and said, 'He's in the workshop. With you shortly.'

'Thanks.'

She nodded and went back behind the counter.

The walls rushed towards him, then away. The floor rose and fell. He searched and found a fixed point in her soft, creamy hands, once more wrapping crockery and silverware in sheets of newspaper. The image dissolved and he flowed deep into the print smudges, oily in the heat, inking the deep creases of her knuckles, a viscous membrane forming on her ring finger, between the gold and the flesh.

She stopped, alert like a bird on a branch.

He snapped back into himself.

She placed her bits and pieces in a grimy waxcloth bag, walked to the front door, turned and called towards the back, 'Jack, customer. Trunk.' Another nod and she was gone in the tinkle of the bell above the door.

Jack came in from the back, trailing dried dirt, grinding it into the mat. He wiped his hands on his cracked, red-brown leather waistcoat and baggy trousers thick with paint and wood stain.

'You're interested in the trunk?' Jack stood, feet wide, wiry arms folded across his bony chest.

'Yeah.'

'Any particular reason?'

'Packing up.'

'Right.'

'How much for it?'

'Everything in your wallet.' Jack grinned like flint.

'I think you saw me coming.'

'Maybe I did.'

A thin trickle of blood ran down his forehead.

'You're bleeding,' Jack said, fixed to his spot.

'Am I?' He wiped it away.

'What happened?'

'Think I got hit with a spade.'

'Was it trying to get your attention?'

'Is that funny?'

'I'm not laughing.' Jack looked deeper, sniffed closer. 'Heavy night, was it?'

'All the way to morning. And a bit more.'

'One of those, eh? Still, a blow to the head can be a dangerous thing. We should get you to a hospital.'

'No.'

'Sit down then.' Jack gestured towards the yard.

'No.'

'As you wish,' Jack said. 'What's your name?'

'What's yours?'

'Jack Cronin. Yours?'

He offered a blank face.

'Have you any identification? A wallet maybe? In your pocket there, for instance?'

He pulled out a leather wallet and handed it to Jack. A piece of white card, torn at one corner, a dry nail of Sellotape clinging to the ragged edge, fell to the floor.

What's that? Not money. Can't matter.

Jack placed his foot on it and pushed it under a small side-table. He then pulled out a bank card and a credit card.

'William, is it?'

'What?'

'According to this, you're called William R Deal.'

He thought for a moment. 'Bill,' he said. 'Call me Bill.'

'And what's this?' Jack took out another card. 'You're an actor? Fully paid-up union member.'

'That's right.'

'Noble profession.'

'Some say.'

'And some don't?'

'Everyone's a critic.'

'So, you remember that much?'

'It comes and goes.'

'Does it indeed?'

Jack slipped the wallet into the right-hand pocket of his waistcoat and walked to the front door. He locked it, flipped the sign to 'Closed' and pulled down the blind. He took some coins from his trouser pocket and dropped them into a glass sweet jar sitting next to a small silver bell on the counter.

'My wife...' Bill lifted the knife off the mantelpiece.

'What about your wife?' Jack fixed one steady eye on the knife, and the other on Bill.

Bill set the knife back on the mantelpiece.

'You really should get to a hospital,' Jack said.

'No.'

'Not keen on hospitals?'

'Like that's a bad thing?'

'Could be, in the circumstances. Unless you're the kind of man who'd rather be dead and buried before he even knows he's ill. Are you that kind of man, Bill?'

'I've no idea what kind of man I am.'

'I see.'

The room began to dissolve again, and himself with it, his thoughts seeping into the coarse pores of Jack's lean face, rancid as old butter on a dirty dish.

Jack wiped his cheek with his cuff, and tucked greasy stragglers behind his ears. Bill felt saliva rising, an acrid whiff triggering a tiny electric spasm in his throat.

Fuck, he reeks.

Bill tasted sugar, salt and something like burnt rubber rising up from his own hot skin, and something else too, something metallic – the tang of iron.

'Tell me,' Jack said. 'What else do you remember? As it comes and goes?'

'I remember lying in the dirt. Something green hopped onto my face and woke me.'

'Something green?'

'A frog. Maybe a frog.'

'So maybe not a frog?'

'Maybe.'

'Uh-huh,' Jack said. 'Anything else?'

'A swing close to a tree and a man looking over the fence.'

'Young? Old?'

'Not that young, not that old.'

'Did you know him?'

'Don't think so.'

'What did he want?'

'No idea.'

Bill lifted the knife again. 'Where do you get all this stuff?'

'House clearances, gutted buildings, skips, contacts, the recently bereaved. I restore bits, sell some as found, do what's needed—'

'All in there?' Bill nodded towards the workshop out back.

'Not everything. I have a factory shop down by Old Street—'

'Where did you get this?' Bill waved the knife.

'We need to get you to a hospital.'

'No.'

'Then let me fix you a drink,' Jack said. 'I have just the thing. I was just about to have one before you arrived. I like a good drink on a long summer's day. Cools me down. It'll cool you down, too. Steady your nerves, clear your head. Help you get home under your own steam.'

'No.'

'Just the one. I can't stay long myself. It's time to shut up shop.'

'No.'

'Hair of the dog. Bite it in the balls. Show it who's boss.'

Bill shook his head.

'You'll come to no harm.'

Bill lit on the words. Jack, he decided, was a dirty little man. 'I can look after myself,' he said. 'I'm not that weak.'

'I'm sure you can.' Jack's mouth pencilled itself into a thin, dark line.

'My wife…' Bill said again.

'What about your wife?' Jack asked again.

'I better go.'

'One drink.' Jack turned and walked out into the yard.

Despite himself, Bill followed him to the back step.

'Sit,' Jack said, rattling free a light aluminium chair from under a battered heavy-metal table that fitted, more or less neatly, into the coolest corner of the small, off-square yard. He picked up the stained, lumpy cushion, snapped it tight and punched it flat. He pulled out another chair and did the same.

On the table sat a scratched glass and a full bottle of cloudy, light-brown liquid.

'No,' Bill said, turning away.

'I'll get another glass.' Jack slipped off his waistcoat and hung it over the back of his chair. 'One drink won't do you any harm.'

Bill made for the front door, managing just a few steps before the room sucked itself into a hole. He crumpled to the floor, clutching wildly at the Chinese screens collapsing around him.

Happy hour

Bill woke up, shaking, saliva running down his chin, moistening the crust already formed. He curled his tongue, stuck it out and tasted the air, licking warm beads of moisture off its taut surface, stretched like plastic to bursting. Sensing a blanket over him and a pillow between his head and the ground, he jolted upright and patted himself all over. He summoned his feral brain to scout for cuts, tears and bruises – anything that smelt strange or off.

For a moment he hung suspended in a grey-white blindness, panicking as a succession of filters rattled across the lenses of his eyes, self-selecting, adjusting. Slowly, the frames overlapped and aligned, the yard sharpening into focus.

No sign of Jack. On the table sat the bottle, two glasses and the knife.

He turned and looked up. A light went out above, followed

by deliberate footsteps on the stair. Jack emerged out of the doorway like a developing print.

'Welcome to happy hour.' Jack slipped his mobile into his trouser pocket.

'So you did call someone?'

'Yes.'

'Who?'

'A very friendly woman.'

'Dropping by, is she? To entertain us?'

'No,' Jack laughed. 'Though it could be very interesting if she did.' He sat down, lifted the bottle and poured a little into one glass. 'It was business.'

'At this time?'

'The work's never done.'

Bill went to stand but his legs refused him.

'Everything still intact?' Jack asked.

'How long have I been out?'

'An hour. Longer.'

Bill sniffed his hide, and then the blanket. 'Is this clean?'

'Clean enough.'

Throwing the blanket off, he dragged himself closer to the table and pawed at the chair.

'Need a hand there?'

'I can manage.' He righted himself just long enough to drop heavily onto the chair and take a breath.

'That's it,' Jack said. 'Get comfortable. Relax.'

They eyed each other in silence, a smile twitching at the corners of Jack's mouth.

'So, what's this then?' Bill asked. 'Your big night in?' Then he groaned as a needle drew a thread of pain through the back of his eye.

'Sounds bad,' Jack said.

'Maybe I should get to a hospital. Thing is, I don't think I can walk far.'

'I could always call an ambulance?'

'No, best not.'

'Best you rest and keep warm then. This stuff will perk you up.'

'Make me feel better, will it?'

'It'll make you exactly what you are.' Jack smiled, eyes like nails. 'Maybe you'd like to wash your hands.'

Bill looked at the blood and dirt on his hands, half stood, lost his balance and dropped back onto the chair.

'Maybe later.' Jack lifted the empty glass, tapped the side with a hard yellow fingernail, poured and set it down for Bill. 'Cheers.'

Bill eyed the drink with suspicion.

'Do you live close by?' Jack asked, pointing suddenly, vaguely, towards Angel station.

'Could do. What's it to you? Do you?'

'Used to. Moved on.'

'Good for you.'

Jack smiled. Bill didn't.

'I notice you're not wearing a wedding ring,' Jack said.

'What?'

'You mentioned a wife.'

Bill had a think. 'I think I threw it away.'

'Did you have a row?'

'Can't remember.'

'Do you fight a lot?'

'No,' Bill said. 'She's good as gold normally.'

'Is she now? You remember that.'

'Memory comes and goes. And, yes.'

'Yes what?'

'Yes, she is. Good as gold.'

'Well,' Jack said. 'To your wife, wherever and however she is.'

Bill stared at the table.

'No? What shall we drink to then?'

'Let's drink to this.' Bill lifted the knife, balancing it on his fingertips.

'Why not?' Jack raised his glass again.

They chinked glasses and drank. Bill choked as the fire of it set his chest alight. The aftertaste was like fungus or wet wood, something rotten. As the heat of it passed, his body cooled, loosening rivulets of sweat from his chest, neck and armpits. No mistaking it, he had to puke.

He staggered towards the back wall. Legs straight, he jack-knifed at the waist, lashing the tiles and the thin patch of soil by the wall with the rope of vomit that twisted its way out of his innards.

Relieved, he sat down. Jack was gone. He reappeared suddenly with a bucket of water.

'What the fuck was in that drink?' Bill asked.

'An old recipe refined over many years.' Jack emptied the bucket onto the steaming tiles.

'Where did you get it?'

'An old friend travels widely. He keeps me well stocked.' Jack grabbed Bill's wrist and checked his pulse. 'Give it a minute and you'll be ready for another.'

'Another?' Bill took a long, deep breath.

'Feel it yet?' Jack asked.

'A bit.'

'Scared?'

'A bit.'

'It'll pass,' Jack said. 'Now, tell me. How did you get that scar on your forehead? And the one on the back of your head?'

'Cop a feel while I was sleeping, did you?'

'I had to dress the wound.'

Bill set the knife on the table, reached around and felt fresh bandaging on the back of his head.

'Don't worry. It's nothing serious. Must have been a very polite spade,' Jack said. 'Still, you're very accident prone.'

'And you're quite the nursemaid,' Bill said, angling the blade towards Jack. 'Where did you get this?'

'It belonged to a young man I knew. A young man called Jon.'

'Is that right? What's the story with him then?'

'Oh, he got himself into a whole heap of trouble, not of his making, you understand. At least, that's what he'd say. If you were to ask him – if you could ask him – it's a fair bet he'd lay the blame at Peirce's door.'

'Who's Peirce?' Bill took another sip, relishing now the slow, strange burn.

'Ian Peirce, his next-door neighbour.'

'And what did he do?'

'He did what everyone does,' Jack said. 'He died.'

A bit of a shock

The first Jon knew that his next-door neighbour, Peirce, had died was when he heard the police breaking down the door one evening, shortly after he got home from work.

'Dead?' he said to one of the policemen. 'When?'

'Two days ago, twenty-first of March,' the policeman said, unblinking. 'Killed himself. Threw himself off the bridge in Prague, up by the castle I think it was.'

'That's a shock.'

'Did you know Mr Peirce at all?'

'Vaguely. We spoke from time to time. He always seemed…'

'Yes…?'

'Like he always had somewhere to be, something to do.'

'Like what?'

'I've no idea. I didn't really know him. I know he was of German extraction.'

'German extraction?'

'And proud of it.'

'Oh,' the policeman said, nodding. 'Did he tell you that?'

'Yes.'

'So you did talk?'

'Rarely.'

'German extraction.' The policeman scribbled in his notebook.

'Now that I think of it, he had mentioned that he was going to Prague.'

'Won't be coming back though, will he?' the policeman said at last, brightly – a bit too brightly.

'Not even to be buried?'

'They'll need to find the body first.'

'The body?'

'No sign of it.'

'If there's no body, how do they know he's dead?'

'Stands to reason.' The policeman pushed out his bottom lip.

'I see what you mean,' Jon said, not seeing it at all.

After the police had secured Peirce's door and gone, Jon left for Mark's studio, even though he knew Mark didn't like him – or anyone else – turning up unannounced.

They had been together for about eighteen months. Mark had come as a total surprise to Jon.

That, people told him, smugly, is how it's supposed to be. They had met at a party. Jon liked Mark immediately, which worried him. He'd learned that it wasn't always good for him to like people immediately. Mark told him he was an artist. Jon told him he wrote. Business, healthcare, corporate communications, that kind of thing, he added quickly, concerned he'd sound boring.

'It pays the bills,' he said, the words big, unapologetic and empty.

'Do you want to do something else?'

Jon instantly read 'else' as 'better', but shrugged as if to say he was fine with it. It was important to let people believe he liked what he did. He'd learned that too.

They slept together that night. Jon told him that he was mentally ill.

'You get straight to the point,' Mark said, after a moment.

'I didn't want you to think I was boring. Artists hate boring people, don't they?'

They stared at each other.

'Am I ugly?' Jon asked, suddenly.

'No,' Mark said.

'But I'm not beautiful.'

'No, you're not.'

'But not boring?'

'Worryingly not. So far.'

'What do I look like then?' Jon asked.

'Like a person.'

'Like how a person imagines?'

'No, like how a person is.'

'How disappointing.'

'If you say so,' Mark said. 'So, what's wrong with you exactly?'

Should he tell him about the Doorman and the rest? Not yet.

'I have fits. I get irrational. Sometimes, I see people who aren't there.'

'Are they nice?'

'Not usually.'

'Do you take anything?'

'Pills.'

'Do they work?'

'When I take them.'

Mark thought for a moment. 'I'm a bit moody myself,' he offered, at last.

And then they had sex again, like hungry people with no manners.

Jon didn't think they'd see each other again, though Mark had suggested it – maybe precisely because he'd suggested it. But they did. Mark took him to his studio that first time, a great cavernous space in an otherwise deserted industrial space by Old Street. He lived there too. It was a mess, of course.

Mark worked with heavy, base materials, mostly stone. Not fashionable, Jon thought, but then what did he know? Well, he knew he liked it.

Don't say that though, whatever you do.

Mark wasn't that big – slight in fact, masculine yet pretty. His work, however, showed real strength and purpose. Jon assumed there must be anger beneath that.

'I like working with stone,' Mark said, smiling. 'I like turning it soft.'

Jon came to need that smile, but noticed, too soon, that he saw it less often.

That, people told him, even more smugly, is how it's supposed to be.

Jon quickly drifted away from a lot of the people he'd known before and saw no reason why Mark need ever know too much as long as he kept taking his 'meds'.

So, all things considered, the 'bad patch' was definitely behind him. No more intense conversations with caring people in pastel-coloured rooms. Work had never been better – too much, if anything – and the debts were slowly shifting. All was fine.

The frictions and calibrations of their relationship were in place before they knew it. This was disappointing. It confirmed Jon's suspicion that if you want to like people, you're better off not getting to know them. But too late, he was already locked in, addicted to patterns of pain and reward.

They indulged in haphazard afternoon epiphanies of alcohol, drugs and sex, sweet and sharp, before sleep, dislocated and careless, on sheets twisted into salty tourniquets. But there were also sullen opaque evenings, ugly mornings and narrow late-night escapes, some of them bodily and bloody, from gutters, roadsides and oncoming traffic.

Whatever the tenor, one thing was consistent – Jon wanted. He did not know why or what, simply that he wanted. He assumed he wanted Mark because, for some reason, Mark was still there. But surely not for much longer? And so he wanted him all the more.

'What do you want exactly?' Mark asked once, in puce frustration.

'Another life,' Jon said, snatching the thought out of the dark. Oddly, it seemed to fit.

'How would you know?' Mark asked, no less frustrated. No less puce.

What Mark wanted was enviably clear: to do his work and live largely untroubled. He had his appetites though. They were plain to see for anyone who looked. Jon looked. He saw them. Then told himself he hadn't.

With Jon's thirty-fifth birthday approaching and Mark's work going well – money in fits and starts, the occasional grant, a substantial sale here and there, the odd handout from Jon – they'd even begun to talk about finding a place together. He was sure they had. When Mark made a big sale, Jon immediately saw an opportunity for a double celebration. Jon Young and Mark Fludd invite you, and all that.

'They'll say it's a wedding,' Mark laughed.

'Let them.'

Mark didn't reply. He often didn't reply. Jon knew to change the subject. Let's just plan the party, the silence said. Forget what it signifies. No, in retrospect, forget *that* it signifies – anything at all. That was probably closer.

The party was just three days away, so it must be wrong that he questioned his right to reach for the buzzer marked 'MF, Artist'. There was a telling pause when Mark heard the voice on the intercom, but he buzzed him up anyway.

Jon waited in the darkness for the lift, the dusty silence suddenly disturbed by industrial whirring and trundling. That always made him feel anxious, uneasy that it would draw attention from someone lying in wait on the stairs – the winos or the druggies who got in from time to time.

Mark stood with his back to him, looking down, in the middle of a pile of circular and oblong stones, weighty brutes all.

'This is new,' Jon said.

'Yes.' Mark dried his hands on an old rag, without looking at him.

'What are you going to do with them?'

Mark glanced towards a crumpled sketch on his worktable, a rough diagram in stubby pencil of four corner pillars and, within the square they formed, three more in a triangle. At the centre of the triangle was one final solitary pillar. The entire arrangement was enclosed in a circle of stones and pebbles.

'Maybe you should paint them,' Jon said, 'in bright colours, you know, like classical statues before they…'

Big mistake. He'd learned, being around Mark and the people he knew, that they never welcomed an idea or a suggestion. If they liked it, they wouldn't admit it. Even if they did admit it, they certainly couldn't use it, so had no reason to be grateful.

No, the way it worked was this: they had ideas and he did not. What they wanted from him, if they wanted anything, was not ideas or approval or even understanding. His interest, preferably silent – awed if he could manage that – would do. They hoped he'd got that, but they had an uneasy feeling he hadn't, that he just couldn't get it at all. Or, worse, pretended not to, just to annoy 'they'.

They were too right.

Jon had also noticed that, in their company, Mark's accent travelled further east, depending on how close 'they' were to the imagined centre – of art, access and all that.

'Next stop, East Ham,' Jon once blurted out, to blank looks all round.

They loved it, of course. Not because they were taken in, but precisely because they knew how bogus it was. Bogus was kosher. It sealed an understanding of unspoken rules.

And when 'they' weren't around? The soft-spoken librarian's son, raised upwardly mobile here and there between Hackney and the borders of Islington, loosened his glottal contortions and relaxed his pose.

'I'm not going to paint them,' Mark said.

'Of course not. Don't know why I said that.'

'I'm going to coat them in animal fat.'

'Animal fat?' Jon stood there, in faint hope of an explanation.

'Yes, animal fat.' Mark's tone signalled that none would be forthcoming.

Don't need one, eh? Even silence could travel east.

I'll bet you're not. Bet you said that just to let me know you have ideas of your own, thank you very much, and it'll be a long time yet before you come begging.

Jon nodded, looking, he hoped, suitably impressed.

'I've just got to…' Mark nodded towards the bathroom. 'Sit down. There's beer and wine, and stuff…'

Thank God for 'stuff'. How many evenings were made more tolerable by 'stuff'?

Jon sat on the sunken sofa and reached for an open bottle of red wine sitting on a heavy trunk now acting as a coffee table. It, too, was new and looked like it was made out of lead. On one side, low down, there was an odd set of markings, an equation perhaps, or a formula of some kind.

On top, pushed to the far-right corner of the trunk, something caught his eye: a bone-handled hunting knife on top of a pile of letters, mostly bills, mostly unopened.

He liked the look of that.

At the sound of the shower convulsing into life, he sank back into the sofa. At times, in the right light, the studio could seem grand and enveloping. At other times, its dust-bowl grubbiness was everywhere he looked.

The kitchen's steely minimalism sulked in a corner beneath greasy dullness. The sink was generally full of half-swilled coffee mugs, and the plughole clogged with dregs. A blackened frying pan, its surface blistered like a mouthful of gum disease, was usually in evidence.

For all its tiles, mirrors, discreet lighting and style-magazine aspirations, the bathroom already stank of mould for lack of a window, its once crisp, vertical lines sagging with damp.

The rest, apart from where Mark worked, was mainly empty space that fizzed with dormant irritation, bristling invisible. The red-and-black Chinese screens added a touch of antique elegance, a hint of division between the bed and the rest.

At the far end, there was a small, rectangular room, more of a cell really, with plain concrete walls and a solid wooden door, always shut.

'What's in there?' Jon once asked.

'Shameful, dirty things,' Mark said.

Jon hoped that, when they lived together, Mark would find somewhere smaller, somewhere just for work. But, as Mark frequently reminded him, the place was cheap.

The owner, so the story went, had left in a bit of a hurry when some business venture went to the wall – he'd gone back to Poland, or somewhere in Europe, he wasn't sure. It might be sold from under him any day. But Mark wasn't bothered. Enjoy it while it lasts, he'd say. He'd find somewhere else when he had to, he assured him.

He was assured all right, for Mark moved in the sort of circles where things could always be found. So while it awaited a buyer and a new purpose, some bright-eyed, entrepreneurial reinvention, it suited Mark's needs perfectly. And, as it was only about fifteen minutes from the Angel, it more or less suited Jon too.

The bathroom door opened and Mark stepped out, wearing baggy linen trousers. With new sweat already blistering his red-white flesh, he screwed the twisted finger of a balding towel into his ears, snapped it in the air and rolled it around his head. Then he sniffed it, squeezed it into a ball and fired it at the bathroom door. He sat at the other end of the sofa, rubbing his thighs, saying nothing.

Jon filled a glass and pushed it towards him. A fragment of 'thanks' blew off the sill of his lip.

'Where did you find this?' Jon asked, nodding towards the trunk.

'In the basement.'

'What's in it?'

'No idea.'

'Aren't you curious?'

'It's more interesting not to know,' Mark said. 'To leave things to be guessed at.'

'Hasn't that been done already?'

'Everything's been done already.'

'Why bother then?'

'Not much choice.'

There was a silence. Then they both laughed. Maybe, though, only Jon laughed.

'Anyway, I can't open it,' Mark said.

'No key?'

'No lock.'

Then, just to needle him, as if the thought had only just occurred, Mark said, 'Did you know this place used to be a printing works for the Bank of England?'

'No, why would I?'

Mark shrugged.

'There might be money in the trunk,' Jon said, after a pause.

'Is money all you ever think about?'

'I find I have to. No one thinks about it for me. Certainly not you.'

'Old wounds.' Mark tut-tutted.

They sat silent for a time, Jon staring at the wall, Mark thumbing through a glossy magazine.

Stew in it. I don't owe you any apologies. Just for once, let's have a proper row. Let's do some proper damage.

The truth was, though, they rarely rowed, not really, because Mark didn't allow it. His line was clear: few things were worth getting into a fight over, and he knew what they were.

Finally, Mark got up and went off to potter among his stones.

Say nothing. Just leave him to it.

Inevitably, Jon went over to him.

'I'm sorry…' Jon said.

'It's all right. No harm done,' Mark said.

Jon wasn't sure whether that was a question, an observation or an instruction.

'Maybe I shouldn't have come,' Jon said.

'What's the matter?'

Jon told him about Peirce and the policeman.

'That's a bit of a shock.'

'Yes, it was.'

'But…'

'I know, I didn't really know him. It's just…'

Mark reached for Jon and looked towards the bed by the wall.

'Do you know what else this place used to be?' Mark asked.

'No idea.'

'A mental hospital,' Mark laughed.

'Really?' Jon tried for a grin that came out as a wince.

'Yes.'

Mark pulled him closer.

You see, no harm done.

They lay in the dark, a single candle burning on one of the stones. Jon watched over Mark until he slept. When he was sure that he would not disturb him, he wrapped himself around him, fingers spread out to gather in his whole upper body, tense and warm and wiry. He slipped his fingers into the hair on Mark's chest and stomach, curling above the deep bone, and took his animal warmth to his nose and lips, tasting it, breathing it in and out, giving it back in kisses between his shoulders, promising that he would never lose him or let him lose himself.

Jon held him softening into sleep, its rhythmic bands deepening in his chest. He leaned over, took a kiss and held it on his tongue, a tiny parcel of breath.

Here, Jon knew Mark as 'they' did not, and saw what 'they' did not. That he was slender and bruised, slighter in his hands than they could ever imagine. That he was in need of protection.

And Jon, of course, was the only one to give it.

Mark's breath sawed lightly across the pillow as his body cooled and the candle burned to nothing on the stone.

Love belongs to others. But you belong to me.

Eggs

As Jon reached the first floor, he saw Eddie sitting on the mat, with his back to the shut door of his flat, his arms folded in embarrassment, unshaven, a smudged look about him. Sarah must have locked him out – again. She'd be inside now, protecting the children, Laura and Tommy, if not from harm, from foolishness. Relentless, red-eyed foolishness.

A dull flash in Eddie's eyes told Jon that he'd like to talk, but he was tired after a late and fairly indulgent night at Mark's, and a long day at work. He simply nodded and walked on up to the next floor.

He'd barely reached the third floor when the door to his right opened. Well, it had been some time and, as always with Mr Rose, he caught him when he was least in the mood. Like he'd decided that the wrong time for Jon was the right time for him. Somehow, he always knew instinctively when that was.

Mr Rose was, Jon guessed, in his early to mid-thirties. Jon didn't know his first name or much else about him. He didn't appear to have a job of any kind, was rarely to be seen during daylight hours and, as far as Jon knew, had never had visitors in the five years he had lived there. Sarah had once mentioned a guardian – a man called Fisher, a doctor, she said – who dropped by once in a while, but that was it.

'Ah, Jon,' Mr Rose said, stepping out onto the landing, which was unusually brave. Then he just stood there, staring, like some changeling half-life.

'Mr Rose.'

'Jon, I was wondering if, by any chance, you had any…?'

'Eggs, Mr Rose?'

'Yes, eggs. The very thing. How did you know?'

Jon knew because he was so used to Mr Rose's odd requests for eggs that he had started stocking up on them just in case. Sometimes, on those rare occasions that Mr Rose would stick his head out of the door in the daytime, he would ask Jon if, by any chance, he happened to be going shopping and could he, possibly, 'a half dozen, on second thoughts, a dozen, perhaps, if you would be so kind…'

It was as if he also knew, instinctively, when Jon would be going shopping. That was impressive, in its way, because Jon didn't imagine himself to be that predictable.

'How many would you like?' Jon asked.

'Ooh…' The soft lips formed into a squashed oval, his eyes rolling to the ceiling and back. 'Would six be out of the question?'

'Six is fine.'

Jon went upstairs to get them and returned.

'You are very kind.' Mr Rose slipped him some money. He always paid. At first Jon had declined, but it soon became clear that, whatever reason Mr Rose had for not buying the eggs himself, it wasn't because he was mean or poor. He paid over the odds and made it plain from the start that refusal would offend.

Mr Rose's grey-blue eyes wandered off to some place only he was allowed to visit. Jon wondered what went on in there when the door closed. What cooped-up thoughts did he marshal through the night, alone?

Mr Rose cleared his throat as if about to make a speech.

'Well, Jon, what sort of a day have you had?'

'Not bad, though my stomach's been troubling me a little.'

The grey-blue eyes grew large. 'Perhaps you're egg-bound.'

For the first time, Jon wondered whether he was actually making a joke but, searching his expression – his only expression, inscrutable, adjustable, up or down, by only a few degrees – he couldn't be sure.

'I don't eat eggs that often, Mr Rose.'

'Why not?'

'I rarely get the chance.'

For a long moment, Mr Rose gazed at him, quizzically, trying, perhaps, to decipher what he meant.

'Ah,' he said, at last, with great relief, 'of course, you lead such a…' He soared in wide, elegant circles for a moment before landing, startled, on the words '…dreadfully busy life'.

'I suppose I do.'

Then, as Mr Rose gave him another long, looping look, Jon began to feel queasy. Was Mr Rose, of all people – having flickered out of his daily trance just long enough to consider his 'dreadful' busyness – looking at him with pity? A clammy, white anger crawled up from Jon's stomach and rippled across his skin. But, as Mr Rose's look held steady, as blank as it was unnerving, Jon saw that his expression – his only expression – signified precisely nothing.

That's why you do what you do for him – remember. Because attention has to be paid, yes, even to the likes of this shattered soul, who bothers no one, except you. And for what? A few eggs, whatever he does with them to soothe his compulsions.

There should be more like him. At least he keeps himself to himself.

There'd been an awkward silence, so Jon said, without thinking much about it, 'Terrible news about Peirce, isn't it?'

'Peirce?'

'Yes, the man above you – my next-door neighbour. He died in Prague. Didn't you know him?'

'Oh no, I don't really know anyone now.'

No, don't imagine you do.

'Well, it is late.' Mr Rose retreated, the hint of a curtsy in his backward step.

'Goodnight.'

A final, graceful bow and the door closed.

Jon went on up to the next floor. It was only then he

noticed that the boarding on Peirce's door had already been removed. As Jon closed his front door behind him, he could have sworn he heard Peirce's door quickly open and, just as quickly, shut again. He listened in the hallway, in the darkness, but heard nothing.

He watched the late news with practised suspicion, had a bath, drank some wine, despite feeling queasy, and went to bed. But he couldn't sleep, with the voice in his head, the old familiar voice, repeating, 'I hate you. I really hate you.'

He sensed a presence, the old familiar presence, at the boundary of the bedroom door, so he slipped his hand under the pillow and held tight the bone-handled hunting knife, which he had slipped into his pocket while Mark was sleeping.

In the morning, he woke, not wanting to or much able to, sick and tired before the day had even begun.

Quid pro quo

Bill's dead aunt eyed him with disapproval and winked. Her face slipped sideways and another slid into view.

After the second glass, he hadn't immediately thrown up again. He now closed his eyes and everything turned upside down. He could see the insides of his body. Liver, pancreas and spleen formed a fist to punch his stomach and lungs into his throat. Out it came, blood-red scalding jets tearing through his throat and nostrils, ripping out his sinuses and rattling the cartilage.

'Don't resist it,' Jack said. 'Don't try to direct it. Let it do what it has to.'

He nodded, trying to understand.

'Stop vomiting now. Here, rinse and spit,' Jack said, handing him a glass of water. 'Don't swallow, just rinse.'

'I'm so thirsty.'

'I know, but don't drink it.'

He rinsed, spat and shot thick streams of snot out of both nostrils. Jack handed him tissues, roughly bunched, a workman's posy.

Slowly, Bill felt calmer, though not well enough to walk. Kaleidoscopic images pressed through the pink of his eyelids, but the nausea had passed, giving way to light, shivery warmth. Opening his eyes, he sensed presences left and right, and somehow he knew that they were paying close attention to everything going on between him and Jack. As he focused on two entwined snakes tattooed on Jack's forearm, they flowed in and out of each other, detaching themselves from the flesh to hover, plastic and vivid, illuminating the air from the inside.

As Jack talked of Jon and Mark, Pierce and Mr Rose, his words twisted around themselves, conjuring and projecting sound and four-dimensional images, and more, into some shared space that existed inside, between and around himself and Jack. At times, his own thoughts took on visible form or coalesced into musical notes and vibrations that, he now understood, had always existed and would never end. He could not tell whether Jack was speaking or sharing Jon's story with him merely by thinking it. He was not even sure whether it was Jack who was thinking it or he himself, inhabiting it – maybe even remembering it.

The image of Jon, waking with his hand on the knife under the pillow, faded. Bill found himself present in the yard once more, with Jack staring at him.

'You look frightened,' Jack said.

Bill nodded. The presences he had sensed earlier had kept their distance, but now they gathered closely around the table. He looked to his left, instantly dissolving the shared space between himself and Jack. And there she was, his dead aunt.

One face after another slid into view, each flickering fully into form, briefly demanding his attention for reasons he did not, or would not, understand. Some he knew and some he recognised. Others were complete strangers who peered deeply into him. One, with black eyes and yellow-grey skin, looked like he would have his hide for gloves in a heartbeat. Another was all compassion, sweet as pale butter and summer afternoons. Somehow, he knew them all, even those he didn't. But he didn't want to look at any of them, because that would be to acknowledge them, and to acknowledge them would be to give them power. He turned and focused on the back wall.

It stood on all fours, staring straight at him.

'What do you see?' Jack asked.

'A big red fox,' Bill said.

'Ah, the fox.'

'He looks old.'

'He's very old.'

'Friend of yours?'

'Old friend.'

When the fox was sure it had Bill's attention, it turned, deliberately, and started digging in the thin patch of soil that ran between the edge of the tiles and the wall. Bill watched as it tore at the earth, uncovering a soft, white bundle. He got up and walked down the yard. He looked down at a baby wrapped in a blanket, a tiny teddy bear in its arms.

'What is it?' Jack asked.

'A dead baby,' Bill said.

'Whose?'

'My wife's. She had a miscarriage. Sudden. Didn't even think it was serious. Just looked down. Saw a tiny red spot on the white of her panties, she said. But that was it. Next thing, she's in hospital. And it's gone. Dead. They told me. Over the phone.'

'Who told you?'

'Helen and Jez.'

'Who are they?'

'Friends. Of hers. Not mine,' Bill said. 'Interfering cunts.'

'And why did they tell you?'

'Because they took her to the hospital. She called them, you see. Not me. They'd just gone by the time I got there. Good thing. Anyway, the nurse tells me she's sleeping, too tired to talk to anyone. Not too tired to talk to them, though, I say. She doesn't answer. I'll just leave this, I say. Leave it on her pillow.'

'Leave what?'

'Little teddy to make her feel better when she wakes up.'

'What's her name?'

Bill hesitated.

'You still don't remember?'

'Laura.'

'Is it now?'

'It is.'

'And where is Laura now?'

'I don't know.' Bill turned. 'Tell me more about him.'

'Who?'

'Your mate Jon.'

'Why?'

'Tell me more about him, and I'll tell you more about me. Maybe.'

'Quid pro quo?'

'What?'

'Deal.'

'Yeah, deal.' Bill turned again and looked down. The fox was gone. There was no hole, no baby, no teddy.

'Tell you what, though,' Bill said. 'I could do with another drink.'

Babysitting

Sarah caught him napping. A knock at the door was rare. Jon thought it might be the police again, so he opened it without checking.

'Eddie and I are having a night out,' she said. 'No big occasion. Just need a break.'

'Of course. Who doesn't?'

He saw immediately where it was heading but no handy excuse presented itself. So there he was the next night, the on-call babysitter, thirty-five feeling all of fourteen. The instructions were pretty simple. Tommy, five, was already in his pyjamas. He could stay up for an hour before bed. Laura, who was twelve but looked older, was happy enough in her bedroom. She'd sort herself out for bed by ten, Sarah told him. She'd be no trouble.

'We'll be back by twelve,' Sarah said.

'No problem,' Jon said.

'There's snacks and wine in the kitchen.'

'OK, thanks. Bye.'

'Bye now.'

The door shut.

Tommy sat on the sofa next to Jon.

'Do you want to watch TV?' Jon asked.

Tommy smiled, shook his head and waved a crayon.

'OK.' Jon smiled back.

Tommy started drawing in his sketchpad, glancing shyly up at Jon once or twice. Then, he seemed happily lost to himself, so Jon left him to it.

Eddie's guitar was propped up against the wall in a corner. His old record player was still mounted vertically on the wall – and it actually worked. At least, it used to. Jon was very impressed the first time he saw that. Anyone who can do that, he thought, must know a trick or two. As he quickly discovered, Eddie knew a trick, but not two. That was it, the full repertoire.

He felt a tiny tug at his arm and Tommy moved closer with his drawings. One was a window in a simple room, looking out onto flat land, trees in the distance. The other was a mass of faces, white, flattened orbs with thick black outlines, features barely suggested by dashes and blotches, all swimming in a clotted mass of red and black.

Jon found one touching and the next disturbing.

'They're good...' Jon said. 'What are they?'

Tommy started to describe them. At least Jon guessed

that's what he was doing. He couldn't really understand what he was saying.

'That's fantastic,' Jon said.

Tommy offered him a crayon and patted his sketchpad.

'I don't think I'd better draw in your book. That's your book, that's Tommy's book. I don't think your mum would like me drawing in it.'

From Tommy's look, Jon wasn't sure whether he'd confused him or disappointed him. Thinking quickly, he said, 'Tell you what, it's nearly time for bed. How about I read you a story. Yes?'

That seemed to work. Jon carried him to bed, tucked him in and started reading. He'd done this before, so he knew Tommy's favourite books, or at least the ones that used to be his favourites. He put on the different voices and made him laugh.

When Jon had finished reading, Tommy told him that when he grew up, he was going to be a farmer – there was a farmer in the story. Each time Jon saw Tommy, he'd tell him what he was going to be when he grew up. And each time it had changed, freshly minted, not a vein of doubt.

'A farmer – that sounds great. That's a good plan,' Jon said, just as he always said. 'You'll be a great farmer.'

'Yeah.' Tommy clapped his hands in front of him, jiggling from his middle.

'Time for sleep.' Jon patted him on the head.

He was relieved the boy was happy. Other times he'd seen him, his face was in shadow, confused and needy. Jon held him once when he cried. He never figured out why, but his little heart was breaking, he knew that much.

As he was closing Tommy's door behind him, he saw Laura come out of her room and make for the bathroom.

'Everything OK?' he asked.

She gave a tight nod.

Never had much to say to him. Never asked anything of him or, he suspected, of anyone else. Tougher than Tommy, that was clear. Maybe because she got just enough love before it ran thin and was smart enough to know it couldn't run any thinner. Only twelve, but already had a look that said her bag was packed and ready. Just as soon as it was legal, she'd be off.

Pretty, too, but wore it like she feared it didn't belong to her. Head always inclined to one side, as if hoping the prettiness would slip off and she wouldn't have the burden of it anymore.

'She's a good girl,' her mother would say of her – flatly, routinely, within her earshot, little noticing, Jon thought, how each time it seemed to tighten a suffocating band around the girl.

True enough, around ten o'clock, with a brisk goodnight, Laura went to bed. Jon opened the wine, and eked it out for the next two hours. True to their word also, Sarah and Eddie arrived back just before twelve.

'All quiet?' Sarah asked in a half-theatrical whisper as if, after just one evening out, all the rules had changed, and they'd stumbled into an ideal home with its very own home-baked nuclear family.

'Yes, fine,' Jon said.

'Another drink?' Eddie asked.

'Or a coffee?' Sarah suggested.

'He'll have a drink.' Eddie pulled another bottle from the back of the cupboard above the fridge.

'Yes, another, thanks.' Jon pushed his glass across the table.

'I'll just freshen up,' Sarah said, still half-whispering, tiptoeing off to the bathroom.

Eddie sat, pushed his glass to one side and started rolling a joint. Suddenly animated, he shook his head in the direction of his guitar. 'Yeah, got some work…'

The words fell over each other like nervous mice in a laboratory maze, as tobacco, papers and bits of cardboard found their way in and out of his mouth. From what Jon could make out, Eddie was playing support on tour, to someone, somewhere, not quite sure who or where. The story fizzled to nothing in the lighting of the joint.

'That's great,' Jon said. 'When's that?'

He got some mumbled half-explanation. He doubted even Eddie believed it.

'Still, a bit of work's come up,' Eddie repeated.

'You said.'

'Nothing much, a spot of labouring, through a mate, you know. It's all money.'

'Right,' Jon said, wondering whether he should ask how the music job and the labouring job fitted around each other. He decided not to bother. There was no guarantee that either was real.

'All money,' Eddie repeated, sucking hard on the joint, his face as thin as a Friday-night promise, pupils like biro points, oscillating frantically on a surface already scored black.

This wasn't his first of the evening. Jon knew the routine. Sneak out the back, have a quick one, then back in for another pint. And so on.

Eddie offered the joint across. Jon raised his hand by way of 'no thanks' and in a second it was soggy between Eddie's lips again.

You don't look good, Jon thought. You won't live long, and maybe that's for the best. You're lost, and unlikely to be found.

Eddie let loose a snake of smoke that rattled its dirty tail in his chest.

Sarah came back into the room, looked at Eddie, then at Jon, her face like weak tea. She rubbed freshly soaped hands together and sat down opposite Jon.

Eddie's eyes rolled, their vertical hold broken.

'You're done, Eddie. Why don't you go to bed?' Sarah said, with neither contempt nor compassion, both long exhausted, and little else left.

Eddie grunted, squashed the powdery-grey stub in the ashtray and hauled himself forwards. With his elbows on his knees, he finally yanked himself upright.

'Right then, goodnight folks.' He wobbled towards the door. 'Oh and thanks for…'

'No problem,' Jon said.

'To the new millennium,' Eddie said.

'The new millennium.' Jon raised his glass.

A glance at Sarah brought nothing in return. As soon as Eddie was through the door, she got up and shut it tight.

'I'll be off,' Jon said.

'No, finish your drink.' Sarah sat side-saddle on the arm of the sofa, in her ghost of a dress, drawing a cigarette from her pack without even lifting it from the table.

A few puffs in silence, then she cast her eyes down, hard enough to drill through the floor.

Jon tugged needlessly at the tops of his trousers.

'I wish to Christ that overgrown child would grow up, stop fantasising and get himself a job. I swear I don't know what to do sometimes. I really don't,' Sarah said suddenly. 'I've enough to do looking after two real children. Thank God my mother looks after them after school so I can get out to work. I couldn't trust him. I couldn't. That's the truth of it. Isn't that a terrible thing to have to admit?'

Terrible but true, Jon thought.

'And the cost of childcare, Jesus. Anyone who can afford it doesn't need to work.'

True again, he thought.

'Honestly, if my father hadn't died and left a bit—' The words lost their shape as her face turned grey-white, like cold mash in an old pot. 'I don't know how I'd cope sometimes.'

Not strictly true, Jon thought. You're not coping, plain and simple. At least, you won't for much longer. Of course, he wouldn't say that. He couldn't say that.

Say nothing. That is both wrong and right. But for the best.

Should he tell her, though, about Tommy's drawings? They suggested, maybe, that all this – this business between her and Eddie, the strain, the worry and the rows – was affecting Tommy more than she realised.

Not now, he decided, imagining her pained look, as fingers of smoke curled out of her nostrils to point right back at him in accusation: what the fuck do you know of such things, such pressures – what it's like to be a mother struggling to do her best?

Fuck all. But then I didn't invite myself. I'm leaving anyway—

Sarah jumped up and prowled the room, tidying things that refused to be tidied, more in the hope, it seemed, that they might become something else, be somewhere else. She scratched at the crude tattoo of a dove on her upper left arm, with 'Eddie' etched underneath, as if trying to tear it out of her flesh.

For a second it looked as if, just maybe, she believed some great hand might reach out of nowhere, grab her by the neck and snap her and her children into a spin in some other – any other – direction.

She looked at him, lifted a cushion and dropped it back in the same spot, conceding defeat. No hand, no spin, no other direction.

'He's such a useless fucking…' The words bubbled red and black in her half-open mouth, as if the cigarette smoke had turned to glass and shattered.

She's not expecting anything spectacular, is she? Not like

she's hoping he's going to bag CEO of some multinational. No, just something steady, a bit of regular money would be nice for a change. Who couldn't see that? Eddie, apparently.

'I'm sorry,' Jon said.

'It's not your fault.'

True, but that doesn't help.

'It's late,' he said.

'I suppose it is.' She absently smoothed the cushion.

At the front door, Jon turned and she gave him a half-hug.

'Thanks for babysitting,' she said. 'It was good to get out.'

'No problem,' he said. 'Any time.'

She shut the door and he took a moment to loathe how he pitied her.

Back in his flat, he sat up late, drinking more and listening to music until he fell asleep on the sofa.

Woken by a bang on the wall from Peirce's flat, he sat up. It was already morning. The banging continued, sharp raps at regular intervals of a few seconds, and then came a muffled voice, maybe angry, maybe pleading, the words indistinct, their shape looping. He got up, went over, pressed his ear to the wall and listened. After a few minutes he thought he could make out what the voice was telling him:

'He has what you want.'

The exchange

Jon stood staring at the huge dark stain spreading out over the living-room wall adjoining Peirce's flat. He went out onto the landing.

The door to Pierce's flat was open just a crack, and he could hear typing coming from the far end. The door gave easily at his touch and he edged his way in. He walked down the long hall-way towards the half-open living-room door and marched in.

A man was sitting at a desk, banging away at a keyboard. He was heavy set, jowly, with greying hair sticking up on either side of his head in stiff wings. He wore a pale, baggy linen shirt and matching trousers.

He definitely looked like Peirce. Only, at the same time, he did not.

'For a dead man,' Jon said, 'you're a very inconsiderate neighbour.'

'I'm not your neighbour,' the man said, turning his head to blow enormous smoke rings at the wall, flicking ash at an overflowing ashtray on the desk. 'I'm the playwright.'

The smoke rings hit their target and seeped in, the stain visibly darkening.

'A playwright?' Jon asked.

'*The* playwright,' the man said, blowing out more rings.

'What is that disgusting stain?'

'I can't decide whether it's art, rage or cancer,' the man said.

'It's spread to my flat.'

'Well, complain to the management, not me,' the man said, pulling a face and taking a swig of cloudy drink from a large glass. 'Care for one?'

'It's a little early, don't you think?'

'It's never early. It's always late. Later than you think.' Big, throaty laugh.

Jon stared at him.

'Well you'd better come in as you're here,' the man said. 'And close the door. I never could stand a draught.'

Jon did as he asked and the man motioned for him to take a seat on the sofa.

'Are you Peirce?' Jon asked. 'People think you're dead, you know.'

'I'm not Peirce,' he said. 'I'm Herman.'

'Herman?'

'Yes, Herman.' He sucked hard on a freshly lit cigarette and blew out another enormous ring. 'This man Peirce, did he go to Prague?'

'Yes.'

'Ah, yes, makes sense.'

Jon wasn't seeing it and Herman knew it. Seemed to be enjoying it, in fact.

'Have a drink,' Herman said, pouring more of the cloudy liquid into another glass. 'I insist.'

Jon hesitated but then accepted. He took a mouthful. It was peculiar and had a slightly bitter aftertaste, of fungus or wet wood, something rotten.

'I also went to Prague,' Herman said. 'To meet Mercer.'

'Mercer? I'm sorry, who's—?'

'He has what you want,' Herman said. 'He had what I wanted. And no one wanted more than I wanted.'

Jon took another slow sip and waited.

'I was a waiter,' Herman said. 'A waiter who wrote a play. A cliché, a genius. I laboured over it for years, in grubby obscurity. And I despaired.'

'Despaired?'

'Have you ever waited tables?'

'No, I haven't—'

'Didn't think so. You wouldn't ask if you had,' Herman said, his eyes large and watery. 'Sodding tables, stained with food and drink and ash and spit and vomit and Christ knows what. Shitting pigeons, begging your pardon, have better table manners than most people. Especially when somebody else gets to clear up after them. The dirty-arsed bastards. Wouldn't know a tablecloth from a toilet roll.'

'I see,' Jon said, the drink's fire setting his chest alight.

'You can't begin to imagine how much I hated them,' Herman said, rubbing his hands, warming to his theme. 'Night after night, expecting me to attend to their needs. Opening their cuckoo mouths, demanding and consuming until they were too bloated to move. If I'd funnelled shit down their throats, pardon me, they'd have let me, their lips never done smacking for more.'

Herman placed his fingertips together and drummed them under his chin, clearly relishing the thought, the coated tip of his tongue protruding from his puckered lips.

The room was getting hotter. The hatred in Herman's throat vibrated, like some hot, dirty machine distorting the air into haze. The sweat poured down his face and rose up, sparking on the silver-blue air, translucent flies frying in electric traps.

'Most of all I loathed those self-important bastards who'd labour over menus, asking, "What's this then?" and "What would you recommend?", as if I remotely cared to tell them. Recommend? I recommend you order and shut up before I get creative with the cutlery and stick a fork in your eye. Pop your orbs out onto the Caesar and croutons, I'd think to myself. How's that for a recommendation, you poncey fucker?'

Jon shifted forwards on the sofa, his breathing shallow.

'Oh, pardon me,' Herman said, getting up and heading into the kitchen. 'I'm forgetting my manners. You'll be wanting to vomit.'

Jon fell to his knees, hands splayed. Herman set a basin on the floor, knelt beside him and held his head back as he let loose the contents of his stomach.

'That's it, get it all out,' Herman said. 'All done?'

'I think so.' Jon wiped his mouth.

'You see,' Herman called out, as he rinsed the basin in the kitchen, 'the thing that really got me, really got me, was that they never questioned their right to any of it – their beautiful homes, their overpaid jobs, their clothes, their expensive evenings out, their lovers, their families, their—'

He stopped to compose himself.

'They never doubted that they meant something, that they amounted to an existence, that everything that could be had was theirs for the asking, and that they, irrefutably, were – and mattered.'

Jon sank into the sofa, letting aftershocks of nausea diminish.

'Give it a minute,' Herman said. 'Then you'll be ready for another.'

'Another?'

'Yes, two is all it takes,' Herman said. 'So, where were we?'

'You despaired.'

'Ah yes. I had written a play, but I despaired it would ever see the light of day, until I got the message.'

'The message? Who from?'

'From Mercer, of course'

'How did you get the message?'

'Well, I had sunk very low indeed. My father would have been delighted to see what I had become. "Look at you, with your smart uniform and everything," he would have said. "Coooh, who's a pretty boy?" He'd have been so thrilled. Not proud, you understand, just crowing. Thrilled that servitude had stripped me of any ideas about myself. My father wasn't one for having ideas, least of all about oneself. In his book, nothing could be more corrupting. Not good mental hygiene, he used to say.'

'The message?' Jon asked again.

'Oh, yes. One night, after a gallon of drink in a grubby bar, the voice in my head grew dark. People should stick to what they're good at, it insisted, and not get mad ideas about themselves. What would happen if we looked to the playwrights to put food on our table? I've no idea, I said. We'd all starve, that's what. And then it laughed, a vicious, filthy laugh, like a sewer having a great big shit of its own. Pardon my Prussian, but imagine such a thing. Anyway, you're proof, the voice said, of the danger of confusing the stage with the table, one thing with another. Of not seeing clearly. Then it told me what to do.'

'And what was that?'

'Slit my throat. Best place for you, the grave, it said. So I felt for the pocketknife I always carried and slipped into a cubicle. I stared at the blade and readied myself. To take hold of the material of the moment and shape it for ever. Do you know what the material of that moment was?'

Jon shook his head.

'Crisis. The material of the moment was crisis. And crisis is made of danger and opportunity. I'd felt the danger but now I glimpsed – something helped me to glimpse – the opportunity.'

'What opportunity?' Jon leaned closer, glass in hand.

Herman paused, reached for the bottle, poured him another drink and watched contentedly as he sipped it, this time with less revulsion.

'The opportunity signalled in the tangled net of graffiti on the door. There, slowly, out of the casual apocalyptic foot-notes and the everyday scrawl of bestial filth, it revealed itself to me.'

'What did?'

'A message that I should meet Mercer in Prague, for the exchange that would transform my life. I was to meet him in a bar up by the castle. On the evening of the twentieth of March. So, I went. He'd been expecting me. Recognised me immediately, of course. We exchanged warm pleasantries and had drinks. I told him about my play and he agreed on the spot to produce it. It all went very smoothly.'

'So, he's a producer?'

'Oh, he has many arrows to his many bows – property, buying and selling, this and that, and all over, too. His energy and industry are astonishing. He's had business interests in Prague for a long time, and an apartment there. A beautiful apartment.'

'He invited you to his home?'

'Yes, after the bar, to continue drinking. We sat at a long table made out of wood – box, I think. The walls were deco-rated with ceramic tiles, colourful, fiery, depicting strange animals and fish, surrounding huge mirrors. We talked and drank until morning. He's a fascinating man, a marvellous conversationalist. He introduced me to this.' Herman wiggled his glass.

'I see.'

'The next morning, I walked back out into a Prague that was exactly the same. Only, at the same time, it was not. The city burned under a new sun. I sat at a café in the shade, drinking coffee and iced drinks, tasting them as a baby first sups, watching mothers and children playing in a pool, in a moment never before witnessed. I tell you, I was made of diamond, and the rough unmade world could not cut me. If I'd walked into the sunlight, I would have blinded people. When it got cooler, I took a tram – of bright new metal – up to the castle, just as it was the day before, identical, yet different in every stone. I saw an excited crowd gathered by the bridge. They were pointing at the water below...'

'Where Peirce threw himself off?'

'Yes. Then my phone rang. I answered it. It was Mercer. He said it was time. So soon? Yes.'

'For what?'

'For Peirce to exchange his life with mine. I took the flask out of my pocket, pulled out the stopper and drank.'

'What flask?'

'The crowd pressed tightly at one end of the bridge. I heard a woman cry out as she slipped into the tangle of their feet. A man tore into the knotted limbs to drag her free. Another woman watched him in horror, looked at me, then back at the water and then, again, at my face. I felt her confusion. I knew she had recognised me...'

'Because you looked just like Peirce?'

'Only, at the same time, I did not.'

'And then?'

'I put my hand in my pocket for my wallet, to get a taxi, to get away. Attracting attention like that wasn't smart. When I pulled it out, it felt different – a softer leather, a smoother skin. When I checked inside, I remembered.'

'What?'

'That I was Herman. That I'd always been Herman.'

Jon nodded. 'And where do you think Peirce is now?'

'Sitting in a room that may or may not be like this one, talking to someone who may or may not be like you, about matters that may or may not be the same.'

'And what happened to the woman?'

'What woman?'

'The woman who fell.'

'What odds?' Herman shrugged, lighting another cigarette.

Jon went to get up. Herman, with an upturned hand, motioned for him to stay.

'So, you see, you have to meet him,' Herman said.

'Mercer?'

'Yes, Mercer.'

'Why?'

'Because he has what you want.'

'And what's that?'

'Another life, of course.'

'So I should go to Prague?'

'No need. He's in town. He runs The Panharmonium

Theatre, at the back of the Green Lion on Birkenhead Street, just a few minutes' walk from here. That's where my play is to be staged.'

Jon set down his glass. He felt a dull pain, a familiar brown fug whispering around him.

A man, who runs a theatre a few streets away, inviting someone to meet him in Prague, by means of a message, left randomly where anyone could see it, in a toilet, in another city?

He knew this well. The impeccable shot logic, the extravagant implausibility tortured into coherence, delusion snapping at the heels of reason, breathless and full of longing. He feared it. Yet, it seduced him. Because he knew, after all, what many did not: that reason and delusion are the fondest of kissing cousins.

The brown fug diffused into bright yellow, silver and white, before evaporating to hang, ecstatic in the air, compressing oxygen into jewels, light into stained glass. Time sliced itself into cross-sections, like wafers of skin that he could pick out and rest in the palm of his hand. Every detail was vivid, surrendering layer after layer of meaning, an infinite regress, held and understood in a single thought. Just as long as he didn't think about thinking.

Herman watched Jon staring wide eyed at the palm of his hand and asked, 'Do you embrace people?'

'What?'

'Do you embrace people?'

'I embrace some people.'

Herman drew deeply on his cigarette, searching him closely. 'A lukewarm embrace, I think. Lukewarm in action, intense in feeling. A dangerous combination. You know where that leads.'

'Do I?'

'To romantic notions. To binary madness. To love versus the rest, and nothing in between. To cataclysm. To crises. And we know what crises are made of, don't we?'

Jon nodded. It now made perfect sense.

'And we don't want that, do we?'

Jon shook his head.

'Do you embrace Mark?' Herman asked.

'Yes, of course I embrace Mark.'

'When's the party?'

'Tonight.'

'Oh dear,' Herman said, blowing even bigger rings at the wall. 'It will all end badly, you know.'

A bit queer

Queers just seemed to like him, he said. He didn't know why. Kept coming at him, all his life, out of every cupboard.

The paramedic in the ambulance paid no attention as he washed away the blood and checked for wounds. All the time, the policeman kept watch. Go on, any excuse, his eyes said.

Must have been just after he first came to London that he met her. The returning soldier, discharge less than honourable. Drugs in the locker, second offence, last chance.

Thanks for that, Queen and country. After all I did for you, eh?

That was '97 or '98. Round about then. Dates get fuzzy.

He'd come to stay with a mate, Ben, who had a flat in Greenwich. One bedroom, sofa bed, wasn't much, but it was a start. He only had his kit bag. Anyway, one night, for a change, Ben suggested they go to a pub in Blackheath.

The Falcon, was it? The Falcon and Cap. That was it.

'That's a songbird,' Ben told him.

Ben knew about that stuff. He was a bit soft, Ben, truth be told. A bit queer, he always thought. Knew him from back home. Dartford? Maybe Ilford, all gets a bit blurry. Wherever the fuck. Anyway, Ben was the last friend he had before the rabbit and the wall going up and all of that.

There was that Friday night, lying on their backs on the heath, drunk – well teenage drunk – on a couple of bottles of cider, looking up at the stars, talking about girls. Thing is, he was talking about girls. Ben was listening, but he just had this feeling, first time it came to him, from the look in his eyes, that Ben wasn't thinking about girls. Ben was thinking about him.

He didn't think much of it. Didn't much care, just as long as he kept his hands off, didn't expect anything because, you know, he wasn't going to be able to help him out with that.

Sorry Ben mate, you're on your own there.

Then, not sure what happened. Went home probably. Never talked about it. And nothing did happen. Ben wasn't the type to try anything. Wouldn't dare. He was a bit, you know, gentle. They still knocked about together, until his dad put a stop to him seeing anyone, that is. Little Benny, hanging around for the taste he'd never get. That he knew he'd never get.

Is that what you liked, Benny? Torturing yourself? Did that make you feel nice? Bit tingly inside, eh?

The more Ben hung around, torturing himself, the more

he started to enjoy it. Enjoyed giving Ben what he wanted, by not giving him what he wanted. Made him hard, he suspected. Ben that is, not him.

Poor Benny with his lonely stiffy. Never getting a sniff.

After a while, he reckoned, every time they met, Benny would go home afterwards and smack his cock off the bedroom wall, thinking about him until he shot his dirty water all over the Dulux. Peppermint green it was, if he recalled correctly. Very popular, back then. So that would have shown. His mum would've noticed that. Not nice. She would not have been pleased. You had to laugh.

Of course, Ben wasn't the only one. They seemed to like him, for some reason, queers. There was the man at the fairground who offered him a watch for a suck in the toilets. Then that other one, in his twenties maybe, peering down over the top of the cubicle, giving him the wink. The social worker, the manager of the local supermarket. Honestly, over the years, he'd lost count. Queers coming at him, out of every cupboard, they did.

Anyway, after the army, he needed somewhere to stay. Just for a kick-off. He'd heard, from someone who knew someone or something like that, that Ben was in London. So, got his number, tracked him down. Ben wouldn't say no. Besides, it definitely wouldn't be for long. He didn't want to end up sleeping too long on a queer's sofa bed. He wanted a place of his own. He wanted the best. He was moving up in the world.

So Ben had got into birdwatching. That was a laugh, when he thought about it. And he was always trying to get him to go with him, for some reason. Maybe he hoped they'd go wild in the country or something.

'Birdwatching? Who does that? No thanks, mate. I'll stick with my survival training if it's all the same to you.'

So, this night, in they went to the Falcon and Cap. He's not sure why now, but he was all dressed up – suit, collar, cufflinks and best tie. Beautiful, even if he did say so himself. Last thing his mum gave him before he left home, that tie. Diamond-patterned, silk. Red, black and white lines, criss-crossing. The shapes they cut. And the red, like thick syrup it was. Like the stuff you used to get on ice cream, from Mr Whippie in the van. You could almost lick it. Lovely.

She liked it too, Yvonne. Liked it the moment she saw him in it, she told him later. She was always ready for it when she saw him kitted out in his best. Couldn't resist, she said.

She made a beeline straight for them.

'What can I get you, gents?' she said, eyeing him up and down. Served them all evening, she did. Always straight in there before anyone else had a chance.

'You play hard to get, don't you?' she said.

He shrugged.

'So do I,' she said. 'But I always win.'

And she did. Well, he let her think she had, for as long as it suited him. She had a few years on him. Ten, she said. Probably more, he thought.

She kept herself trim. Nothing had moved south or any-thing. He admired that. Snappy little purse on her too, tight clasp, considering she'd done a fair bit of shopping, he reckoned. Took a strong thumb, he used to say. And tongue. And jaw. She'd picked up a few tricks along the way, so that made for a more attractive package all in all.

She was an actress, she told him. Wore a fur coat. Fake, of course. Fair enough. Bit parts here and there. Bit of modelling when she was younger. Some hand modelling too. Well, she knew how to use them.

A few weeks later and he'd moved in with her. Few months later, following year maybe, he married her. Nothing fancy, registry office job. Reception at the pub, free champagne before cracking open the Scotch for a proper drink.

So there he was, married to her, running the pub with her.

'I'm knocking slices out of her, day and night,' he told Ben, one evening when they went out drinking. Different pub, of course. Had to have time off. Might get lucky too. Wouldn't shit on his own doorstep, would he now?

Ben lapped it up, not saying much, just getting hotter and hotter under the collar. He reckoned it turned Ben on, just thinking about him giving it to Yvonne. Just thinking about him giving it to anyone.

Poor little Benny. Still tormenting yourself? Still not getting a touch? Bless.

'She can't control herself. Can't get enough. Sucks me dry, she does,' he said. 'Sometimes, busy lunchtimes, right, she'll say, "I don't feel too well. It's you. You're making me ill. You're giving me a real headache. I need to go and lie down for a bit." That's my cue, see. The punters downstairs, they're sticking daggers in each other's backs for a drink, one barmaid rushed off her feet, pretty little thing too, while I'm up in the back room giving her a good seeing-to. Tell you what, though.'

'What?' Ben asked, face all flushed, loving it he was.

'She really is all fur coat and no knickers when I'm around. She fucking loves it.'

They had a right good laugh.

But time passed. Not much time, true. Still, things got stale, quickly. Of course, he didn't give up just like that. He reckoned you had to put some effort in. Work that bit harder to keep it interesting. They'd made vows, after all. That stood for something, didn't it? It's supposed to.

They tried games, role-play, instructions, rules, duties, obedience, knowing your place, taking responsibility for yourself and what you do, or don't. Discipline, taking the punishment you deserve, just like in the army. Holding your face up to the light for a good slap when you know you've done wrong. She was ready to go a long way for him. You know, memorise the rules and do all the necessary. Fair play to her, she tried. But it was time to get serious.

The rules. He drew them up. Wrote them down. All the do's and don'ts.

More time passed. The list of rules got longer. She had trouble remembering. Well, she was knocking on a bit. And, of course, if she couldn't remember all the rules, she couldn't obey them all, could she? And if she couldn't obey them all, he just had to discipline her more often. And, well, he had to admit he did get a bit carried away sometimes, when he was, you know, drunk. Very, very drunk.

71

Terrible truth was, though, he was bored with her already.

'No man wants to fall down on the same mattress his whole life, does he?'

Ben shrugged, trying to change the subject. Was it Ben he told that to? To be honest, could well have been someone else by that stage.

He did the only honest thing he could do. She'd arranged for them to go on holiday. He thought she thought it'd calm things down a bit. By then, though, he'd gone right off her. Calming down wasn't what he needed. He needed tuning up.

'I didn't even like the taste anymore,' he said. 'And when the taste's gone, it's time to move on.'

Someone nodded back, whoever it was he was talking to. Some punter, some freeloader, some twat, probably.

So, he looked for an excuse to have an argument and come back early. He told her he was going on one of his survival weekends. He needed a little time to himself to think things out, clear his head.

When he got back, he took what was in the till, packed a bag and left. Made straight for his bolthole.

'Hello Benny,' he said. 'Invite me in then, mate. Don't leave me standing on the doorstep. Don't worry. Won't stay long. Just until I get myself sorted.'

He never saw Yvonne again. Never gave her much of a thought after that, to tell you the truth. Saw no need. She'd had her portion of him. If she felt a bit peckish, she'd just have to order something in, wouldn't she? Wasn't like she didn't know how. She'd be all right. She'd find something. Get by somehow. Her type always did.

Anyway, got divorced. Took a while. She wouldn't give in at first. Probably thought he'd come back. Then it finally dawned on her she'd had the last she was getting off him. That was Yvonne all over, though. No real sense. Most of them don't, though, do they? See what they want. Hear what they want. That's why they need someone strong to take charge.

The money didn't last long, of course. Time to get another job. With his army background, security work made sense. He still knew some people, made some calls. Worked at the MoD building in Whitehall. And the Old Admiralty Building. Parliament too. Bit of painting and decorating, on the side, here and there. Old Street, one job, as it happens.

Then he moved up a bit. Doorman at some exclusive clubs, one in Notting Hill and one in – South Kensington was it? Then, chauffeur – proper uniform job. Peak cap. The works. White shirt, perfectly turned cuffs and collars, smart jacket, pressed trousers, double-heeled socks – just like his mum used to knit for him as her way of, you know, saying sorry or something, like it could possibly make any difference by that point. You could've snipped a lady's panties off with the crease in his trousers.

Somehow he lost it and things started to slide. Ended up in a homeless shelter. Not sure where, somewhere in central London, probably. Dinah's, that's right. Dinah's Diner. Poetic that. The homeless loved a bit of poetry, he found. Especially on the underground, stomping ground for poets and pickpockets. Handy that. Made a killing on the Piccadilly line for a while.

He liked it, at the shelter, the diner. Felt at home there, he did. Well, he was at home there. He'd nowhere else by then. Cleaned himself up a bit and got a job in the kitchen. Worked all hours. Not sure why but went through a bit of a phase when all he wanted to do was work. Needed to keep himself busy. Keep his mind off other things. Day and night, he worked.

And then he got the sack. Someone told the guy who ran the place he'd called someone a queer.

He might have done but not like that.

'I don't hate queers,' he said. 'Look at my mate Benny. I don't hate him. I just don't like what they do. Men's arses weren't meant for that, were they? If they were, God would have given us a zip there, wouldn't he? Or some sort of slot and Velcro arrangement. They should keep that stuff to themselves. Not go around shouting about it.'

You had to laugh. They were both laughing now. Dirty, filthy laughter. Pissing themselves, they were.

Then he just stared at the ground. At the paving slab. Like a sheet of paper, it was. The black worms wriggling. Just like in the front room. Standing by the piano.

Where was this now? That's right. On the little square just by the church. He'd moved again. Gone down in the world. The Drop-In, King's Cross Road. He kept staring at the slab. The worms wriggled, grew and crawled towards him.

Think of the face, taking its last look in the mirror. Think of all the reasons he's given you to hate him. Punch the face. Punch it again. Punch it into a pulp. And when you know the face can't take any more, punch it again. Take your time.

Who was he talking to? Not Benny, no. Well, of course not Benny. He was talking about Benny. Not to Benny. Talk fucking sense.

Benny, the flat in Greenwich, the sofa bed, all long gone. No forwarding address. No number. Where was Benny? Dead or something? Someone said he'd seen him. Said he'd gotten very thin. Not long, someone said.

So, who was it he was talking to? Some drunk, some druggie, some cunt with bad teeth down from Glasgow or the North? Some ginger Paddy just off the potato boat from Ireland? Getting friendly, queering him up. And laughing at his mate Benny? Not fucking having that.

He broke the neck of the bottle on the edge of the bench.

'Queers. Out. Of. Every. Fucking. Cupboard,' he repeated, over and over, to the paramedic, who could find no serious wounds. Not on him anyway.

The policeman said something he couldn't make out into his walkie-talkie. Didn't take his eyes off him, though. Not for one second. Any excuse, his eyes said.

He didn't give him one. Pick your battles. Quit while you've still got your teeth.

He woke up some time later.

'Carry on like this and you'll be dead in months,' the doctor said, like he didn't care much either way.

No arguing with that.

The day he was discharged, on his way back to King's Cross Road, dry, hollow and shaky, the world too close, too loud, too bright, he looked up as he was rolling a fag. Saw a sign for an acting school. Pictures of people off the telly outside. Cheap, too, it said.

Well, if Yvonne can do it, can't be that difficult. Not like she had much upstairs or anything. Something to do, something new.

He'd look good on telly. Great in uniform.

Just ask Yvonne.

The Two Eagles

It all ended badly. When Jon woke up, his mind was blank. Then, he remembered running water and being carried, a terrible pressure in his ears, not being able to breathe. Then, just going limp. Letting go, strangely relaxed.

His clothes from the night before had been thrown around the room, not folded neatly on the chair as normal. A bag full of presents had spilled all over the floor.

He threw back the bedclothes, turned on the radio and went to the bathroom. He turned on the bathroom light. The bath was half full of rusty-looking water, his torn shirt floating in it. Bottles of aftershave and a large antique jug lay in chunks on the floor.

He stood over the hand basin and looked at himself in the mirror on the medicine cabinet door. From the bedroom, he heard the voice on the radio announce that six people had died the night before in the explosion in Soho and that many more were injured.

Full marks, Mark. No one's love stopped them dying.

He opened the medicine cabinet and searched for pills. Painkillers, something, anything.

He arrived late at the Two Eagles, the stain spreading fast beneath the evening. They were all there, 'they' who actually did things and 'they' who forever hovered around 'they' who did – whatever it was they did.

'Here comes the bride,' Nick called out, applauding himself, as Jon made his way to the seat next to Mark.

Yes, Nick. Repartee reflex fully sprung, shiny and witless, straight out of the manual, every line a carnival float.

Still, they laughed. Nick 'made things happen', as they were never done saying, so they had no choice but to laugh. Jon always suspected that Mark liked Nick's usefulness more than he liked Nick. Matt was better, but only just.

'Are you all right?' Mark asked, pouring him some wine.

'Fine,' Jon said.

'Sure?'

'Nerves.'

Mark nodded. He did not look reassured. He did not look sympathetic. He looked short on patience.

They'd been seated in one limb of an L-shaped section of the upstairs restaurant, away from the other diners, facing grand French windows looking out onto the rooftop garden. On the black-and-white silk tablecloth, single roses, white alternating with red, had been placed in thin, silver vases in front of each place setting.

As the plates were cleared and the drinking went on, people shuffled around the table.

Those women from the gallery. Do they own it, run it or just work there? Maybe they're an installation. That studied blankness could endure for days under a spotlight.

'Mark and I are getting a place together,' Jon said.

'He hasn't mentioned it,' one of them said. 'But then he's very secretive.'

'Oh, that's wonderful,' the other one said, her eyes flitting around the table in search of someone with more influence, leverage, traction, suction, or whatever they were calling it now.

'Are you a good cook?' the first one asked.

Jon stared at her.

'It's just that I've never known Mark to cook anything.'

'Oh, he's hopeless, just hopeless,' said the other one. 'He'd live in a greasy spoon.'

'Haven't you been to his place? He already does,' the first one said.

They laughed. Fondly, was it? He couldn't tell. Everything they said or did seemed to be received, processed and filtered through some neutralising decoder.

'That's right,' Jon said. 'I get to play the doting wife. He gets to leave shit everywhere and be creative. I get to cook, clean up and endlessly adore him. It's been my life's ambition. I'm just waiting for him to sell a couple more pieces for big numbers and then I can take early retirement. Thought I might take a part-time job. In a charity shop, maybe – you know, so I can get to gossip with old ladies and sell scented candles and smelly second-hand pants to the poor and needy.'

They stared, thought about it and decided it was safe to laugh.

'Mark says you write. What do you write?' the first one, maybe the second, asked.

'Articles, brochures, annual reports, that sort of thing.'

'Oh, right. Articles about what?' Her gaze drifted over his shoulder.

'Business, corporate stuff, healthcare – a lot of that.'

'Is that interesting?' she asked, fidgeting with her napkin.

'It pays.'

'Right, it's all money.'

'Yes, it's all money.'

Somehow that conversation rubbed itself into another.

Matt just had to have his say. 'You really don't like Nick, do you?'

Jon shrugged. 'Never thought about it. He's amusing, I suppose, and God knows these troubled times are crying out for quality entertainment. Someone should fund him.'

'Nick doesn't need funding. He's arrived. He's good at what he does.'

'And what is that exactly?'

'He makes things happen. He oils the wheels. You should ask Mark.'

'Yes, he's very oily. Practically self-basting. If we can just find an oven big enough for his head—'

'Why exactly are you so envious?'

'It's not envy.'

'No?'

'I loathe the self-admiring.'

'Not everyone has to be so self-hating. Or so controlling.'

'Some things are best kept under control.'

'Whatever keeps you warm at night.'

'Mark keeps me warm at night.'

'Mark's kept a lot of people warm at night.'

Jon wondered whether now was the right time to punch him in the face. Or did etiquette demand he wait a while?

'You seem very invested there,' Matt said, sensing blood, pressing further.

'He's not a bank,' Jon said. 'Believe me, he's not.'

'Yes, he said you're always fretting about money. Have you ever thought of working for the taxman?'

'Have you ever thought that you and Nick are really about as creative as continental starvation?'

That conversation rubbed out too, into darkening hues.

The evening sped through a miasma of cigarettes and alcohol, played out in negative, as though relayed remotely from some hidden transmitter, mysterious in design, covert in purpose. To Jon, the people at the table seemed barely to exist at all. Behind the talk and laughter hammering the scorched air, a banging voice told him he did not like these people, and that they did not like him; never had. They actively despise you, the voice insisted.

Someone whispered that Peter and Fiona had split up. Someone intimated they'd sensed some tension, but that was nothing new. Someone else said Nick and Matt were taking career breaks and going off travelling.

'What are they going to do?' Jon interrupted. 'Bring home a small country for the spare room? Spend its GDP on soft furnishings?'

Word spread that a bomb had gone off somewhere in the centre of town. Suddenly it was there, unwelcome news on a ripple of agitation from a nearby table. In Soho, someone said.

A cry of delight went up as the waiters carried in on a gold dish a pure white peacock sculpted out of ice cream, decorated with real peacock feathers and surrounded by hot, bright red cherries. They set it down and started serving.

Jon imagined that bomb going off in the middle of them. At the moment of detonation he'd see his mind blown apart, like the chandeliers above them in smithereens, every thought he'd ever had, hanging suspended in the air. And he'd finally see how they'd held him in their intricate patterning, just before they hit the floor with a pop. He felt an urge to run out and find a bomb that hadn't gone off, wrap himself around it and cradle it like a newborn.

Careful, the madness must be showing. Phil the Pill from Notting Hill is looking at me, a bit puzzled, a bit worried, doing his best, as ever, to look a little bit bored. Phil the bloody Pill, with his lazy, calculating eyes, like a stunned lizard, ubiquitous, forever prattling on about some film script he's 'developing' or the band he manages, which no one has ever heard of. Must be Eddie's band.

You're just here to deal drugs. That's why you're always bloody here. They don't like you any more than they like me. But you're a steady supply and for that they're prepared to have you in their homes, cutting coke in the new extension.

Jon laughed loudly for no apparent reason. Phil's eyes flickered over him. Jon returned the look, and then shut his eyes. He saw no chandeliers. He saw only a rusty bedside lamp in a cheap hotel. No bulb, no plug, no point. No way he was paying the bill. He laughed again, a thick, filthy snigger, and opened his eyes. Phil was looking right at him.

Now he's wondering. He hates me but he thinks there's an outside chance, just maybe, that I'm so mental I might buy some stuff, so he guesses I'm worth a sniff.

'No way I'm paying the bill,' Jon said, leaning in closer, tapping out every syllable on the table.

'Seriously, don't care mate. Not my problem.'

'For the hotel,' Jon said, tapping the side of his nose. 'No bulb, no light, no bill. No pay, no way.'

Phil looked like he wanted to hit him. Jon wished he would. There were bombs going off. People were dying tonight. Who'd notice a punch-up and a few overturned tables? Besides, he'd have the sleazy little shit across the face quick enough.

Mark, sensing something not quite right, turned to Jon. 'What's going on?'

Phil gave Mark a tight little 'all right mate?' twitch, muttering 'fucking off his face' under his breath.

'No bulb, no light,' Jon said to Mark, thinking just how much he'd like to smash Phil the Pill's face off the edge of the table, repeatedly, until he heard some bone crunch. See some cartilage fly across the room like castanets, click his heels in glee, make a toothpick out of his philtrum and dance his way home.

Phil made his escape.

'Kiss me like I'm dying,' Jon said.

'You're drunk,' Mark said.

'Love should stop death.'

'Nothing can stop death.'

'Not even love?'

'Not even love.'

'Then love is fucking useless.'

'Everything is useless according to you,' Mark said. 'Maybe useful and useless are the wrong way of looking at things. Maybe, just get used to it.'

'That's not what I want.'

'What do you fucking want, Jon?'

'Another drink.'

'Bad idea.'

He had one anyway.

The evening thickened with threat. Jon looked at Mark and it was suddenly clear to him that they were never going to live together. They did not belong together. They were not together, in any way that mattered, and never had been. And everyone else knew that already.

Just then, someone to Mark's right spoke to him and he

seized the opportunity to turn and chat, sprung free, like a greyhound out of a trap.

Fucker.

Jon's senses fused into one, absorbing everything around him. He saw the words as they came out of people's mouths, spiralling, tightening, coming undone again and shooting up through the ceiling. He smelt a band of yellow on a dress, heard the cherries in the melting ice cream, and tasted the light collecting in pools in the leaves brushing against the window.

He went hot and cold, moist and dry. He spun away from himself and was dragged back. He reached for water, icy and sweet. He gulped it down. Looking up, he saw a grey blur emerge out of the sky, turn black and speed towards the windows. It hit with full force, sending a tremble through the wood, causing everyone to jump. For a second it hung there on the vibrating pane, wings fully spread, before falling to the ground. One of the waiters went out. Several people followed, Jon trailing at the back. It lay there, black, bloody and misshapen.

'Should we call somebody?' someone asked.

Jon looked at its twisted, bleeding body, its matted feathers, its beak opening and shutting, locked in a diminishing loop.

'There's no sense in that,' Jon said, pushing to the front. 'It's dead already.'

He couldn't remember much after that. He didn't know what happened to the bird. A sharp twist of the neck, if anyone had sense. He vaguely remembered a silent taxi ride, staring at the back of the driver's head, imagining it repeatedly crushed under someone's boot.

Next thing, he and Mark were in his flat, having an argument. He couldn't swear to any of it though.

'I'm not enough for you,' Jon said.

'You think that, not me,' Mark said.

'No, I say it. You won't.'

'Why wouldn't I say it, if that's what I thought?'

'Because you mistake indifference for affection. That's why everyone loves you, because you don't love at all. You're exactly the sort of person other people always love.'

'And you mistake love for therapy. And everyone doesn't love me. That's just your way of saying that everyone hates you, or that you think they do in that mashed-up thing you have for a brain. And you know why that is?'

'Well, now I finally know what you think.'

'No, you only ever know what you think I think.'

Jon thrust his face into Mark's. He was something much darker than drunk now.

'You can batter anything into shape,' Jon said, grabbing Mark's hands. 'So, go on then, batter me. Hard as you like.'

'You know what's so tedious about self-destruction after a while? The "self" bit. The narcissism. It's just a big fucking lie.'

Jon paced, in circles. He had almost enough sense to leave, go sleep in the street maybe, but then he was back again, face white, lips blue, short of breath.

'I don't want your affection,' he said. 'I want your rage.

That way, I can be sure you feel something. Don't hold anything back.'

'It isn't me who's full of rage,' Mark said.

'Then why do you never speak?'

'Why do you find silence so terrifying?'

'Because it's full of shame.'

'For what?'

'Use your fists. Go on, batter me black and blue. You do anyway.'

'I've never—'

'Not with your fists, no.'

'Hate yourself, if you want, but don't ask me to,' Mark said, turning to leave.

'Oh that's right. Walk away as fucking usual. That's it. Do what you're good at. Well, go on then. Just fuck right off, you empty, petit fucking bourgeois fucking fake. Oh yes, I noticed the accent wandering again tonight. What was that exactly? Cappuccino Cockney? You didn't get that from your mother. And you are mummy's boy, aren't you? That's it, come on. Get your head right up mummy's skirt. Have a good lick. And then spend the rest of your pampered life pretending you're some horny-handed son of muck.'

'Get help.' Mark's face turned the colour of sick.

'Your art is a bogus pose,' Jon yelled. 'And you know it. Which makes you a cynical, manipulative, arse-licking, money-grubbing whore.'

Mark turned.

'Try. Taking. Your. Fucking. Meds.'

'You. Have. No. Fucking. Talent.'

Mark practically flew at him.

He found some painkillers, swallowed two and closed the medicine cabinet. He wasn't sure whether Mark had tried to drown him or revive him after he'd nearly strangled him. Or if it even happened that way at all. Whatever happened, it didn't matter. He got what he asked for.

The mirror under the strip light reflected back the marks around his throat, his bruised face, the whites of his eyes blood red, and his mouth swollen and cracked. He broke the crust on his lower lip and spat a black-red gob onto the white porcelain. He ran the cold water and splashed it up into his face. It hurt. Everywhere.

Bloody Herman. What was in that fucking drink?

Man of many talents

Bill set his empty glass on the table and turned sideways in his chair, stretching his arms and legs out full.

'What happened to Yvonne?' Jack asked.

'No idea,' Bill said. 'Found someone, I expect.'

'Someone strong like you?'

'That's the ticket. Keeps them right. It's what they like. A firm hand, a few kind words, a slap when it's needed.'

'And when is it needed?'

'Most days.' Bill pushed his glass hopefully towards Jack, who ignored it.

'And yet you married Laura.'

'Oh now, you want to be careful there mate, mentioning Laura and Yvonne in the same breath,' Bill said. 'I might take offence. No comparison. Different league altogether. I knew that the minute I saw Laura. I was pulling pints in this pub, different pub altogether, long time after, and she was out with a couple of friends. You know, giggly girls' night out, eyes wide open, looking, not looking, walking right into things, like they do. Then, next thing you know, there's tears. The other two that is, not Laura. She was different. Anyone could see that. She was with them but she wasn't with them. She knew how to carry herself. Knew how to behave.'

'So, no firm hand needed there then?'

'It's all about the timing,' Bill said. 'Just like acting.'

'Have you done much acting lately?' Jack asked.

'Some,' Bill said. 'Roles are hard to come by. Tough game. Early days. Got any music?'

'You did well there. Considering you were in the gutter.'

'I did do well, didn't I? Music?'

'No.'

'Shame.'

'You like music?'

'Of course,' Bill said. 'I used to be a choirboy.'

'Choirboy, pub landlord, actor – you're a man of many talents.'

'Oh, I've done lots of things.'

'You're remembering a lot now. More come than go, I'd say.'

'It's a puzzling condition. What can you do?'

'Keep it coming?'

'Could say the same to you.' Bill rolled his empty glass in his hand.

'Not yet.'

'Seriously, I'm parched here with all this chat.'

Jack wasn't giving.

'Yvonne? Seriously, what did happen to her?' Jack kept a firm grip on the bottle.

'Honestly don't know.' Bill eyed the bottle, licking his lips. 'Got older, slacker, more miserable probably, paying more, getting less, no idea, who cares? Still, I did leave her something to remember me by. Something to snuggle up to on a cold winter's night. Didn't mean to, mind. I just forgot. I was in such a hurry to leave. Left it hanging in the wardrobe.'

'What?'

'My uniform.'

'The chauffeur's uniform?'

'My soldier's uniform. She liked me in that.'

'Where was it you served?'

'Bosnia?'

'With?'

'2nd Battalion Light Infantry.'

'When?'

'1995, it was, I think. Relieved the 1st Battalion, Devon-shire and Dorset.'

'Memory's definitely getting better. Full recovery on the cards, do you think?'

'Bit of rest and recuperation still needed, mate.'

'Why did you join up?'

'Things got a bit messy after my dad died. I mean, thank fuck he did. Best thing ever happened.'

'How did he die?'

'And this girl, I'd got her up the duff, and I was too young for babies and all that.'

'How did he die?'

'So, I thought to myself – it's a man's world, after all, and off I went. Always someone needs shooting.'

'How did he die?'

'Quid pro quo.' Bill winked.

'Tell me what he did.'

'He was a barber. And a preacher of sorts. A hypocrite. A bastard. And he's dead. Life story. In a nutshell. Moving on, eh?'

Jack rested the neck of the bottle on Bill's glass and started to pour.

'Tell you what,' Bill said, 'be a darling and make mine a double.'

'Careful, you don't want to get ahead of yourself with this stuff.'

'Best place to be.' Bill winked again. Then, something caught his eye. Looking down, he saw, where he'd been lying, a dark viscous liquid, black as ink, bubbling up out of the ground and spreading across the concrete.

'That doesn't look right, mate. Not by any means.'

'It's the drains. It happens in summer,' Jack said. 'Just ignore it.'

'It's spreading. Seriously, though, what is that?'

'Nothing important.'

'Smells like sewage.'

'No, it's not sewage.'

'Smells like it. A bit like it, you have to admit.'

'Maybe a bit like it.' Jack sniffed and poured him a large measure.

The man next to you

Five to ten, Jon rang the buzzer. No response. Above, no lights. He waited for a minute, then went and stood at the other end of the street, where he had a clear view of the studio windows. Mark stood with his back to the glass, undressed to the waist. The man next to him pulled him close.

Jon set off for Old Street station. The tube home was full, the surface of the air razored with bacteria.

A young woman kept an anxious eye on her bags. The young man next to her, salty, hormonal and eager, whispered in her ear. His lip stuck to her lobe. Jon smelt their sweat cooling, alcohol evaporating off their puppy flesh.

Another woman, in her thirties, maybe forties, stared into space, her face a child's toy, eyes, nose and mouth crudely darned in an old sock, a comforter. Her fingers lay upturned on her lap like cold chips on a plate.

She nursed a bruise, like a shadow on an X-ray, sunk deep, pressed early. Someone should attend to her. Protect her. She deserved love, as much as anyone. The man next to her held himself at an anxious distance, nostrils twitching, as if he'd just detected gas.

Jon got off at the Angel.

'Big Issue?'

Grey cigarette flesh, dry and flaking. 'No thanks. Mind how you go.'

He headed for St John Street.

Love must exist. It must save. All the fretting people, tracing and retracing numbing radii, never daring circumference, never imagining surface and light.

He cut around Claremont Square and down through Holford Gardens. The wind in the trees told him: Love does not belong to you. It never will. You are a grub. You achieve no more in living and dying than bisecting the spine of a leaf.

He found the door to the block wedged open. Some of the upstairs neighbours – people he'd never really got to know – were loading bags, cases and boxes into a small van and a car. He looked up at the 'For Sale' sign with the 'Sold' sticker slapped across it. They nodded.

'Leaving?' Jon asked.

'Making a start,' the woman said. 'The big move is in a couple of days.'

'Good luck,' Jon said. 'Hate moving.'

'Thanks,' she said, silently directing the man next to her

to lift a large box of kitchen utensils. He shot her a look that said *only one pair of hands, you know.* They had words Jon didn't catch as he went inside.

On the first floor, a small, soft-grey woman he recognised but did not know came out of Eddie and Sarah's flat. Her mouth drooped on one side, like a tear of treacle through rice pudding. Her eyes were boiled as red as Woolworth's sweets, and she smelt of damp oatmeal biscuits in a tin.

'Oh—' She looked startled.

'Sorry,' he said.

'Eddie,' she said, nodding back over her shoulder.

'Eddie?'

'Bumph,' she said, or something close.

'Bumph?'

'Dead.'

'Oh…God.'

'Sudden.' She patted at her chest.

'I see.'

'Terrible.' Her stubby index finger drew tiny, loose circles in front of her face, in a reflex of grief.

'Should I…?' He nodded towards the door.

'Maybe later. I've just…' The words folded themselves into a tidy choke, the circles tightening above her shoulder.

'Right, of course.'

She drew the back of her hand across her mouth, gave a little cough, a touch rancid, and gathered herself to move around him.

'Sorry.' He rose up on the balls of his feet and pressed

himself into the wall to make room.

'Thanks,' she whispered back, her face low.

'So sorry for your loss.'

What exactly was her loss?

'Thank you.'

She hurried down the stairs without looking at him, gathering herself and her loss in her coat, which was too small and too thin to cover either.

The door opened. Laura stared through the crack. Jon went to speak but nothing came out. She gave him the look he knew well, now doubled in intensity. He nodded. She offered a smile, but snatched it back and shut the door before he could accept it or do anything else with it.

That's Eddie, then. Now he doesn't get a chance to— Do what? More of the same? Nothing measurable.

He went upstairs. Peirce's door had been locked and boarded up. Again.

The stain on the living-room wall had dried out in a dark, misshapen patch. Staring into it, he saw the imprint of a body fallen from a great height. The intricate mottling suggested pulped organs; and the jagged tendrils, shattered, dislocated limbs. Together, they painted a body brutally wronged.

What to do about that? Fresh paint. More money. Not fucking made of it.

He went to the bathroom. The man next to him watched as he searched the medicine cabinet for pills, painkillers, anything.

He found some. He took them.

Drink. There must be something in the fridge. Or the cupboard.

He found a bottle. He drank it.

Lie down and stop. Today is as good a day as any to die. Eddie proves that.

He lay on the bed, clothes loosened, the sash window lowered, and the brown smell of London closing in like an old pub wall on a Friday night. The wash of traffic, near and far, foamed at the pane and retreated, netting in the spume a hard tangle of voices, scissor blades interlocked, grinding to no point. Other voices scattered like pins over stones.

Poor Eddie. Poor Sarah. Poor Tommy. Poor Laura.

The words looped like a transmission that would eventually reach those affected, on some frequency finely tuned for the bereaved.

Outside, a siren child, near and far, cut the slate of evening in two, clean from side to side.

Who attends to the Sock Lady's bruise? No one. It darkens, metastasises. Imbalance perpetuates. Love does not belong to everyone.

He slipped under the rough rim of sleep and out again. Images of the evening replayed, bleached, contrast heightened, demanding some unspecified emotional response or resolution.

Mark is inside me, deep down, enfolded, meshed.

The man next to you wants to give you permission to die. To slit your wrists and bleed into the fracture. If you acknowledge him, you will. It's as good a day as any.

Eyes ahead. Don't look at him.

His right thumb twitched in spasm, triggering a current down one side.

The man at the door hovered, as if to enter. He didn't. He never did.

There was a loud crack, the bedroom burned into negative, and then drumming, softly scattering, rose up in smoke from below.

'We're playing your tune,' the Doorman said.

The icebox

The drumming drifted up the stairwell, its smoky timbre leading Jon to the floor below. The door to Mr Rose's flat was open. It gave easily at his touch and he edged his way in. He looked down the long hallway towards the half-open door of the living room. As he approached it, the drumming got louder.

Mr Rose was stretched out on a crimson velvet sofa, worn mostly threadbare. He was wrapped in a fine silk kimono, loosely belted, frayed and soaked in sweat. He wore a bright red headband and make-up, thickly applied, his lips as crimson as the sofa. Many chairs, cabinets, bookcases and oddments were stuffed into a room too small to welcome them.

Pungent tobacco smoke spiralled from ceiling to floor, barely masking a wet, earthy smell. An ornate wooden pipe lay smouldering in a large ashtray on a small side-table.

On one wall, mounted in a dusty gold frame, the head of a fox, severed in a moment of heightened instinct, observed everything. In fight or flight, it seemed the fight had been lost.

On a broken, high-back chair of intricate basket weave sat a ventriloquist's doll, also dressed in a fine silk kimono, its face made up, lips crimson. Behind it, propped against the wall, between the edge of a curtain and a bookcase thick with dust, stood a broken ladder.

'Turn it off,' Mr Rose said, attempting to throw his voice.

'Turn what off?' Jon asked, placing the back of one hand on Mr Rose's forehead, and two fingers of the other on his wrist, to take his pulse. He was on fire. Jon looked into his eyes but he was absent. Mr Rose said nothing, nodding his head to tell Jon that he wanted him to address the doll.

'Turn what off?' Jon asked the doll.

'The drumming,' Mr Rose said.

Jon found a CD player under folded gold and braided cloths and a heavy candlestick next to a pine cone. He hit the off-button.

Mr Rose's eyes were black pinpoints.

In the bathroom, Jon looked in the medicine cabinet. He found tinctures, powders and lotions, beeswax, Tiger Balm and much more that he had never heard of; some sweet, others pungent, acrid and nauseating, in jars, tubes and small tin pots with faded elegant lettering. He searched medication – orthodox medication, blister packs, crisp pharmaceutical packaging – but found none.

The kitchen was old and shabby, the Formica skin scrubbed to the bone with strong, cheap disinfectant. In the cupboards were more bags and tins of herbs, twigs and bits of things that looked like lumps of old bark and wood shavings.

Jon went back and placed the back of one hand on Mr Rose's forehead. At his touch, he jolted, his eyeballs rolling in their sockets like a hunted animal in a dark wood.

Back in the kitchen, an old yellow fridge rattled and buzzed. Inside, there were eggs on every shelf and even in the cracked salad drawers. Jon tugged hard at the icebox door, trying to force a crack in the white fur that glued it shut. With a squeal the plastic snapped and the door hung limp on one hinge. He dug his hand deep inside, searching for ice cubes. He found none. Scraping all the way to the back, his fingers finally hit something. He pulled out a white plastic box and tore off the lid. Inside, frozen solid, was a human penis.

Back in the living room, he saw that the belt of Mr Rose's kimono had come loose. One swathe of turquoise silk had dripped to the floor, while the other had slipped off the waxy, bony thigh of his upraised left leg and piled itself loosely between his buttock and the abraded velvet.

The wound was old and untidy, a tendril of scar tissue running from his groin into his left thigh. Mr Rose, it turned out, was not Mr Rose, after all. At least, not any longer.

Though the eyes were still black, and the mind absent, the angle of his head had shifted slightly, suggesting he was now beckoning to Jon, like some pallid eunuch coquette.

'Men came,' Mr Rose said.

'What men?'

'Men came. And tore it apart.'

'And tore what apart?'

'And burned it out. Fire in the hole.'

Jon stared at the frozen penis. Unsure of what to do with it, he put it back in the icebox and forced shut the broken door as best he could.

Mr Rose's right arm dangled over the side of the sofa, fingers dripping like curls of cream onto the carpet, his breath shallow but even.

On top of a mahogany writing bureau, jammed between the sofa and the bookcase, lay a battered address book. Inside, in various coloured inks, in places precisely formed and in others misshapen and wild, were many names and numbers, all scored through, sometimes savagely, black lines zigzagging into frenzied densities of ink that in places tore the paper. All were scored out, except one circled in green ink: Dr Fisher.

A guardian, a man called Fisher. A doctor, Sarah had said.

After a quick search, the phone turned up under a pile of cushions. He dialled the number.

'Fisher,' a warm Scottish voice answered.

'Dr Fisher?'

'Speaking.'

'Dr Fisher, I'm sorry to disturb you, but—'

'Has something happened to him?'

'Uh, yes, he—'

'Has he been smoking?'

'Smoking?'

'Stuff. Smoking stuff.'

'Yes,' Jon said, eyeing the pipe. 'Stuff.'

'How bad is he?'

'Very.'

'Is that a professional assessment, young man?' Dr Fisher asked.

'No, I'm not a doctor.'

'No,' Dr Fisher said, almost chuckling, 'I'm the doctor. I'll be right over.' He hung up.

He was there in less than twenty minutes. Jon buzzed him in.

Dr Fisher was tall and broad shouldered. He wore a cream Macintosh and a crisp, chocolate-brown suit in an elegant, classic cut, set against a bright white cotton shirt, and a green silk tie, firmly knotted. His tailored brogues smelt of sweet new leather, as did the large, gleaming case he carried, lightly, in one hand.

What is that smell? Aftershave and Brylcreem. Just how a doctor should smell.

Jon found somewhere to sit and watched as Dr Fisher, on his knees by the sofa, opened his case and took out his equipment. He patted and pumped what life he could manage into as much vein as he could find on Mr Rose's arm and sterilised the injection site. He then broke the tip off a small phial, unwrapped a syringe and drew into it the clear contents of the phial. He injected Mr Rose, withdrew the needle, discarded it with care, and dabbed at the site with cotton wool dipped in sterilising fluid. He discarded it likewise, and taped a small plaster over the pinprick of red.

'That should steady him until we can get him out of here,' Dr Fisher said.

'To hospital?'

'Private clinic. For good, this time. Sadly, I think this independent living experiment has run its course. His condition has seriously deteriorated, I'm afraid. It was only a matter of time really.'

'That's very sad.'

Dr Fisher rearranged Mr Rose's kimono to cover the exposed wound and turned to look at Jon.

'Did you find it?' Dr Fisher asked.

'Yes, I found it. In the icebox.'

'Indeed, where else? And where is it now?'

'Back in the icebox.'

Dr Fisher nodded.

'How did it happen?' Jon asked.

'He attempted it himself – and made a terrible mess of it. You've seen the scar on his thigh, yes? A professional man, colleague of mine, had to make the best of it.'

'Do people normally get to keep it, you know, as a souvenir?'

Dr Fisher gestured all around him. 'What's normal here?'

'Not a lot.'

'Indeed. Old money, you see. Normality, my young friend, is whatever old money wants, if it can afford it. And, usually, whatever it wants is what it can afford.'

'So he's rich?'

Dr Fisher smiled. 'Well, from a rich family, but he's fallen well under the radar. His pot is running low, so I'm afraid we'll have to melt down his assets, so to speak, sell the flat and raid what's left of various guilty trust funds to pay for his care, which won't come cheap, I can tell you. Unfortunately, I don't think he's got long left to be honest. Poor fellow.'

'Is he insane?' Jon asked.

Dr Fisher settled himself into an armchair, took a packet of Camel cigarettes out of his pocket, pulled one out and lit it, sucking in contentedly.

'You smoke?' Jon asked.

'Of course, but nothing illegal or suspect,' Dr Fisher said, taking a deep, satisfying draw. 'You see, he developed exotic and esoteric interests a long time ago. He travelled, the kind of unending travels that only a private and substantial income can permit – far and wide, and deep into other cultures, beliefs and states of mind. He dabbled, experimented, did himself a lot of harm. You might say, he didn't so much cleanse the doors of perception as send in the psychic bailiffs.'

'Exotic and esoteric interests?'

'And old money,' Dr Fisher said, smiling warmly. 'A potentially fatal combination.'

'But why did he chop it off?'

'He got some idea into his head that it would help to purify him spiritually. Cleanse his mind somehow. In his diaries from the time, he wrote that he had to – if I can recall correctly – yes, migrate between sexes, be both male and female, and, somehow, neither.'

'Where did he get that idea?'

'From some shaman somewhere, probably – Peru or Serbia, possibly the Arctic. He met a great many of them. He took substances, met talking plants, spirit serpents, animal guides and daemons. He set out to "fill his cup", his diary said. I believe he overfilled it. It eventually cracked and, well, it's been leaking ever since.'

'And cannot be repaired?'

'Unfortunately not, young man,' Dr Fisher said, puffing away, peering into middle distance.

'I should go,' Jon said, standing up.

'How did you find him?'

'I heard the drumming,' Jon said, sitting down again.

'Hmm, I see,' Dr Fisher said, peering closely now at Jon.

'And what happened to your face and throat, young man? You look like you've been in the wars.'

Jon explained about Peirce, Herman, the night at The Two Eagles, Mark, the argument, the Doorman. All of it.

'Hmmm,' Dr Fisher said again, 'that must have been very upsetting for you. And then to discover all of this must have been, well, very agitating. Do you get agitated?'

'I stay awake for days cooking my agitation. Then I get angry. Then I collapse, usually before I hit something. Or someone.'

'Do you feel agitated right now? Would you like something to calm you?'

'Not sure I would.'

'Let's see, if I can't find something that might just do the

107

trick.' Dr Fisher rummaged in his case.

'I don't think I should.'

'It would help you sleep.'

'I had no trouble sleeping tonight.'

'Really? Then, why are you here? And not in bed?'

'I was in bed.'

'But you're not in bed now, young man, are you?'

'Because it woke me.'

'What did?'

'I told you, the drumming.'

'Ah yes, the drumming.' Dr Fisher took a bottle of tablets out of his case.

'I don't think I should.'

'Why not?'

'I'm already taking medication.'

'And you're taking it regularly?'

'Yes…'

'Which means "no". What are you taking?'

'Olanzapine. Risperidone.'

'Which?'

'Both. I mean one, then the other. And before that, haloperidol. I think.'

Dr Fisher wrinkled his nose and sniffed. 'These are better. They're currently recommended.'

'What are they?'

'Chlorpromazine.'

Jon put out his hand.

'Not so fast, young man,' Dr Fisher said. 'You get yourself

upstairs, clean your teeth and into bed with you. I'll be up in a little while, just as soon as I've sorted things out here.'

Jon nodded and did as he was told.

He lay in bed with the bedside lamp on and the front door closed but unlocked, listening to people moving, with some difficulty, up and down the stairs. As their voices faded, he heard the door to the building close heavily. A few minutes later, an engine revved and the ambulance drove off.

A key turned in the lock below and a steady step made its way upstairs. The knock on the door was low but definite.

'It's open,' Jon called out.

'This is more cosy,' Dr Fisher said, sitting on the edge of the bed. 'You've done well with this place.'

'Thank you.'

'Here are the pills, one month's prescription, which I want you to start taking tomorrow. 'Now, give me your arm.'

'Why?'

'This will calm you and help you sleep, set you up nicely for tomorrow so that those pills can start to do their job,' Dr Fisher said, taking Jon's arm, patting and pumping what life he could manage into as much vein as he could find, and sterilising the injection site. He broke the tip off a small phial, unwrapped a syringe and drew into it the clear contents of the phial. He injected Jon, half-whispering 'there we go, nice and easy'. He withdrew the needle, discarded it with care, and dabbed at the site with cotton wool dipped in sterilising fluid. He discarded it likewise, and taped a fresh plaster over the pinprick of red.

Jon let out a long, deep breath.

'Better?'

'Yes,' Jon said, as mind and body lost all urgency and he sank deep.

'Now, what do you see?' Dr Fisher asked.

'A warm yellow light.'

'Is it the sun?'

'Maybe.'

'And where are you?'

'In a garden,' Jon said. 'The sky is very blue, the sun is a soft electric yellow and the grass as green as plastic. The front door is yellow too, like an egg. My mother is opening it, hesitant, anxious. I don't know where my father is. There is an aeroplane in the sky. I follow its white trail against the deep blue. It is going away. I'm thinking – one day I will get on an aeroplane and go somewhere. There is a man looking over the fence. He sometimes leans over the back fence too. He is looking at me. He looks sad about something. I recognise him. I do not recognise him. He is familiar but different. He tells me that I make mistakes, that I keep making the same mistakes over and over, and that it pains him to watch me do it.'

'Why doesn't he help you?'

'He says he can't help. He says he does what he can. He says I won't listen.'

'To what?'

'To what he tries to tell me.'

'Where is he now?'

'He's walking away. He says he will come back another time.'

'And where are you?'

'I'm on the aeroplane. I'm in the garden. I'm on the aeroplane and in the garden. A different garden, but the same garden.'

'And then what?'

'I wake up in a hospital bed, with a doctor looking down at me. I've had my first seizure, my mother tells me later. I fell and split the back of my head wide open.'

Jon floated up again to find Dr Fisher still sitting on the edge of his bed, humming to himself, the flat of one hand on Jon's forehead, two fingers of his other hand on his wrist, taking his pulse.

'What does it mean?' Jon asked.

'Well, young man,' Dr Fisher said, 'there is an outside chance, I suppose, that he and the other man, the Doorman, are emissaries attempting to lift a small corner of the veil of reality for your perplexing enlightenment, and offer assurance that we are never, ultimately, alone or abandoned. Or, just as likely, they are made of nothing more than the darting lights and escaping gases of the psychic swamp. But whatever they are, you'd best pay them no heed. You'd do better, my young friend, to remember that you are – and there's no gentle way to put this – seriously mentally ill.'

'How seriously?'

'It's as if,' Dr Fisher said, his bedside burr warming, like toffee melting in a pan, 'one night, two liars, each with a different story to tell, simply to entertain themselves and pass the time, caught you in their net and bundled you blind to their place of torture and amusement, where they babbled unceasingly, one into each ear, drowning the middle ground of your mind in a thick black mud of confusion.'

'Can you make me better?'

'I can help you to stop seeing people who aren't there,' he said, patting Jon's arm. 'Protect you from yourself. Now, here is my card. I want you to phone and make an appointment to see me at least one week before your supply runs out. Yes?'

'One week,' Jon said.

'One week before they run out,' Dr Fisher said with gentle emphasis, setting the card on the bedside table, under the lamp.

Jon nodded.

'Now, one last thing,' Dr Fisher said, pulling the white plastic box out of his leather case, opening it and offering him the frozen penis. 'What shall we do with this?'

'You'd better take care of it. I don't think I have any need of it.'

'You're quite sure?'

'I'm very sure.'

Dr Fisher snapped the lid back into place and slipped the box back into his case. 'If you do need it for any reason, you know where to find me.'

'Why would I need it?'

Dr Fisher smiled. 'I'll see myself out.'

As Jon reached over to turn off the bedside lamp, he saw the doctor's card lying there. In sleep's slow, thick enfolding, he picked it up, turned it over and saw that Dr Fisher's practice was on Birkenhead Street.

Summer holidays

He left a bag of hair clippings and other rubbish out back for the binmen. In separate bags, never mixed, do you see? He hosed and disinfected the area, locked the back door, as he must each time, and hung the key on its hook. Where it belonged, you understand. Not in his pocket, never there. Because, at the end of each day, when his father came to retrieve it, that's where he expected to find it. He didn't expect to have to look for it, or ask for it, do you see?

He trudged back into the shop.

'Could your boy run to the newsagent and get me my paper?' the man said, settling back in the big red-leather chair. 'The *Mirror*? And twenty fags? Bensons.'

Who's he calling boy?

His father tensed as he tucked the barber's cape into the man's collar. The man smiled at him, with more taunt than warmth.

His broom slowed to a stop at his feet by a ball of hair clippings, curled like a dead animal on the chequered lino, red, black and white.

Was the man playing games? Did he know? Newspapers and magazines were not allowed. No TV, radio or books either. Well, some books. Those on the Church's list.

He looked to his father for an answer, and his father slapped him with a look.

'I suppose he's too young to buy fags,' the man said.

'Yes,' his father said, short and flat.

'Just the paper then,' the man said, holding out some coins.

His father gave him permission with a tight snap of the neck.

He rested his broom against the wall and took the money.

'The *Mirror*,' the man said, reading in the son's face the father's face.

Outside, he drank down the summer breeze, anticipating the brief release, the joy of springing lightly on the soles of his feet up the High Street.

'Wait.'

He looked around. His father, unable to resist, had followed him outside.

'Tell the newsagent to put it in a brown-paper bag so that you cannot see it,' his father said.

'Yes, sir.'

'And keep it tucked well under your arm on the way back. Don't let anyone see that you have it.'

'Yes, sir.'

'And don't read any of it. Not a word,' his father said, turning and going back inside.

He bounced down the street.

The newsagent's face, as he snapped open the paper bag, told him he'd heard too. Pity or sneer, he couldn't tell. Maybe both.

Back in the shop, he held the bag out to the man in the chair.

'Thanks son,' the man said, raising an eyebrow for his father's benefit at the sight of the bag. 'Just put it on the chair.'

Who's he calling son?

He looked to his father, who again gave permission with a tight snap.

He set the bag down and picked up his broom.

His father avoided catching the man's eye in the mirror, as he made brisk business of cutting his hair, in silence, no chat of the weather, holidays or football, or what a mess the government had got itself into this time.

'Is it clean out back?' his father snapped. 'Lock the door when you're done. And those basins need washing.'

'Yes, sir.'

He rotated the soap dispenser, weighty in its gleaming chrome cradle with its one loose screw, through one perfect loop, and watched the soap fall in thick drops onto his palm. He moved his head back and forth, enjoying the swell and elongation of his reflection in the shiny oval, his face splitting into two huge teardrops.

He drove the soap deep into the creases between fingers and thumbs. The nailbrush stung, as he scrubbed hard, up to the elbows, before rinsing under the sharp jet of cold water. He dried himself with paper towels and dropped them into the bin, the bag folded neatly over the rim under the heavy metal lid.

Before the day was out, he had washed and scrubbed his hands at least a dozen more times, and rinsed basins when they weren't in use, even those that hadn't been used since he last rinsed them.

Today, being the third Tuesday in the month, Cobham Tuesday, 'doing the books' day, as his father shut up shop early, he had, thankfully, less to do than usual.

By the time the school holidays were over, he would have washed, scrubbed, rinsed, swept and mopped hundreds, maybe thousands, of times. And left out back bag after bag after neatly tied bag of hair clippings and rubbish.

At least, after the holidays, it would be back to Saturdays only.

Today, like most days, when he was sure his father wasn't looking, he sneaked a handful of hair clippings into a small plastic bag, which he then folded into as tight a square as possible and hid in his satchel between the pages of his prayer book.

That evening, after he and his parents had eaten and prayed together, he was sent to his room to study. At the telltale sound of dishes clattering below, he imagined the scene. His mother scurrying back and forth between the dining room

117

and the kitchen, while his father sat in his study with his pipe and Bible.

He took the clippings from his satchel and emptied them onto the floor. Unzipping his pants, he masturbated over them. When he was done, he put the clippings back into the plastic bag, sealed it with Sellotape, labelled and dated it, and filed it in date order with the others, in neat rows in his desk drawer.

He honestly can't remember when or why he started taking the clippings out, masturbating over them again and setting them alight on the windowsill, but he thinks it was when the drawer started getting too full. He does know, though, that he just had to know what human hair smelt like on fire.

He established a simple system, keeping each bag of clippings for exactly twenty-eight days before use. After he'd finished, he'd brush the ash off the sill and let the wind carry it out over their garden and the neighbours' gardens and beyond.

He stood at the window and looked upon his town, chest full of air, arms outstretched. How far did it drift and how many people did it touch? How many, without knowing it, brushed it through their hair or breathed it into their lungs and into their blood? No knowing but, however many, the thought pleased him greatly.

He came to believe that he could use the ash to cast spells and curses to be carried on the wind, to settle on people he did not like and people he did not know, who very soon were pretty much one and the same.

One night, when the small plane, as he always remembered it, crashed in flames into the garden next door, he knew that his curse had worked. It angered him later that others remembered only a broken kite, if anything at all. They were wrong. They lied. They did it to spite him. They'd see. They'd learn.

He cursed Mrs Ryan for refusing to give his ball back, scowling over the hedge in her crackling purple Crimplene, her face like the skim of burnt milk, the folds of her throat hanging like shredded beef.

When the news came one day that she had died suddenly in the bathroom, he imagined her on the floor, a look of shock on her face, tan tights around her ankles in a puddle of old-lady pee, feet pressed against the door in her last choking spasm.

He grinned at the thought of her daughter forcing it open, placing a socked toe in the pool of wee, looking around and screaming.

He'd done that too.

After that, he knew he could do whatever he wanted, by willpower, as long as he was up to no good. And that was good enough for him.

No stopping him now. They'd see. All of them.

No stopping him, that is, until the day he arrived home and found his mother waiting for him in his room, the desk drawer open and a handful of blackened matches and ash in her outstretched palm.

'Explain.'

Normally, he was clever and got rid of the matches and the ash. But he must have forgotten. Sometimes he did it in the dark, so maybe he hadn't seen them.

He told her about taking the clippings and keeping them in the drawer, about the dating system and burning them. But not about the other thing. All the same, she looked disgusted, suspicious that there just had to be something more, and that only made her all the more disgusted.

'Your father will have to be told.'

That went without saying.

His father interrogated him, without taking a single breath. The same question, like a machine-gun fired straight at his head, round after round. He knew his father knew for a fact there was something else to it, something unimaginably dirty. He just couldn't figure out what exactly. That could only make it much worse.

The thrashing was brutal. He'll never forget it starting. Never remember it ending.

He woke up in bed, some time later, his father standing over him, holding a small mirror to his face.

'That,' his father said, pointing at a mark on his forehead, 'is the Devil's thumbprint. He came when you were sleeping and pressed his thumb against your flesh, to leave his mark, to let you know that you have sinned and that you are one of his. If you sin again, he will come again, and press his thumb into your flesh again, and mark you again and again until you have no clean flesh left for the Lord to eat at the final feast.'

His father turned the light off and left.

He knew not to turn it on. Or do anything other than lie there until morning.

Next day, in the bathroom mirror, he saw the bruises appearing all over and the mark on his forehead. He didn't remember it being there before. Didn't remember it not being there before.

For a long time after, he'd examine himself for more marks when he'd done or thought something bad. He never found any. It was then he decided to enjoy being as wicked as he could. It was then he decided there was no God, no Devil, nothing but meat, breath and death. His father was just an idiot. A vicious cunt who deserved whatever was coming his way.

At least, come the end of summer, he'd be back to school. Back to Saturdays only in the shop. Couldn't come soon enough.

His father waited until the last Saturday of summer. That evening, after shutting up shop, his father sat in his chair in the study and stood him in front of him.

'I have something to tell you,' his father said.

He waited.

'We've broken away from our Church,' his father said. 'We'll be going it alone now. We don't need them. Their truth is not our truth and the only truth that matters is between ourselves and God.'

He said nothing.

'Also, you won't be going back to school. From now on, we'll be teaching you at home. And you'll work in the shop, Saturdays and Tuesdays.'

He nodded.

'Now strip,' his father said, unbuckling his belt.

The thrashings became regular. For anything, everything and nothing at all. For being bad, because he hadn't learned. For being good, lest he forget. He got a fierce one the day he lost the key to the back door of the shop.

'How could you possibly lose it in under a minute?'

'I put it on the wall there, by the bins,' he said. 'There was a cat. It knocked it off. It fell and went down the drain.'

'A cat? I don't see any cat.'

'It was there. It's gone.'

His father took his keyring out of his pocket, found his back-door key, the master copy, and slid it between the first and second fingers of his fist.

'I'm going to have to pay to have a new one cut from this. Do you see?'

He stood in silence.

His father swung wide and punched him in the side of the head.

He took it gladly, though, and the thrashing too, because he knew, this time, it would be worth every second of the pain.

Bye now

The funeral was brisk and mercifully short on celebratory cant, for which no one had the stomach, imagination or necessary conviction. Afterwards, there was tea, coffee and sandwiches in the flat, with fruit juice and fizzy drinks for the children. No booze, though, much to the disappointment of a few of Eddie's drinking pals, whom Sarah quickly saw off, for good, with a scrotum-shrivelling look, as she stood smoking on the tiny balcony, a perfect study in the convergence of bitterness and relief.

Laura stayed out of sight as much as she could, and Tommy looked confused as he was passed from one person to another. He stayed close to Sarah, except when she was smoking, when her mother or sister Marie would look after him.

He cried at one point, a cry that only children can expel, a deepening hiccup that accelerates into a wail that falls, in time, on its own rocks or is folded into someone's loving cuff.

Poor Tommy, you are loved, Jon told himself, as if it were a transmission that would eventually reach him, on some frequency finely tuned for suffering children.

Jon, having paid his respects, went to say goodbye.

'What happened to you?' Sarah's eyes grew in shock at the sight of his yellowing bruises.

'Jumped in the street.'

'How awful.'

'I'm fine,' Jon said. 'Don't worry. The police are on it. So what now for you?'

'Well…' Sarah said, looking around. 'We'll have to see.'

He had no idea what she meant by that. He found out a few weeks later, when they ran into each other by the door downstairs as he was on his way out.

Tommy was wearing a blue peaked cap and matching T-shirt with a drawing of an onion on it; and emblazoned across it: 'I've got layers, peel me.'

'We've had some good news,' Sarah said.

'Oh yes?'

'We've been offered a new flat. In one of those affordable, social, whatever they're called, I can't remember, housing schemes. Brand new. It's lovely. And there's a park close by. That'll be great for him. Lovely park, wasn't it Tommy?'

'Yes.' Tommy peeped out from under his cap.

'That's fantastic,' Jon said. 'How did that happen?'

'Well, after Eddie,' she coughed, 'and the change in circumstances and everything, I applied. My sister made me. She helped me fill in the forms and all that. She's good at that kind of thing. Knows how to put things. I hate all that. Anyway, because of Tommy, really, I suppose, we were pushed to the top of the list and, well, there you are, we got an offer. And it's lovely. And roomy, isn't it Tommy? You love your new room, don't you?'

Tommy smiled.

'That's fantastic,' Jon said. 'And is Laura pleased?'

'Well,' she coughed, again, 'Laura's not coming.'

'Oh?'

'She could. There's room. But she's going to stay with my sister. There's a better school there that she wants to go to. And I want her to do well at school. And my sister and her husband, they're going to help out. And I think also she just, I don't know, I think…' Her voice trickled dry.

Jon pulled an awkward face that said *no need to explain.*

'I think with Eddie,' Sarah continued, 'and everything, she just wants, I think, she just wants a change really. A few years, when she's got her exams and everything, she won't be long getting her own life started. She's a good head on her. Didn't get it from me. Didn't get it from Eddie, God rest his whatever. Anyway. Takes after my sister, I think.'

'So, when are you going?'

'A week on Friday.'

'So soon?'

'Well, it's ready to move into and I'd be out of here in the morning. I'm not taking much with me. Not much to take.'

'Good for you,' Jon said.

'Right, well, that's us. Better get you fed Tommy, hadn't we?'

Tommy smiled up at her.

She gave Jon an awkward hug. 'In case we don't see you before we go.'

'Take care,' he said.

'Thanks for everything,' she said.

'Didn't do much.'

'You did enough.'

Jon bent down to pick up Tommy, who wrapped his tiny arms around his neck. 'Bye-bye Tommy.'

They turned the corner and disappeared up the stairwell. He waited until he heard the door close above.

Bye Tommy. Be safe.

The swing and the fence

His mother had sent him to the shops to get some things for tea. Ham, a block of cheese, the mild not the strong, and tomatoes – ripe ones, mind, not green.

Sometimes, he thought, she found excuses to let him out when his father wasn't about. At the table, in her robe, not sexy, not mumsy, the same scent always, perfume and animal, trapped in its folds. Her hair down on her shoulders, she'd look at him and pull him in with a guilty smile and her purse, with its promise of chocolate for the walk home.

Chocolate? How old did she think he was? How old did she want to think he was? Still, it was a trip out.

Beyond these secret missions to the shop, he'd rarely set foot outside since he'd been taken out of school. He lifted weights in his room. They were allowed. Because, you know, healthy body means healthy mind and happy hypocrite.

Or maybe he'd sit on the swing in the garden. An old rubber-tyre affair, hanging by ropes from a branch of the tree. He was too old for the swing, but it was something to do. He loved the swing. Otherwise, he'd feed the rabbit. He was too old for the rabbit, but it was company. He loved the rabbit too.

In the street on the way back from the shop, he saw a boy he used to be at school with, heading home from school. A boy who used to knock him about a bit. Not on his own, of course. With his mates, how they do. Because when he was younger, he was a bit on the skinny side, before he filled out and started training.

So he started chatting to this boy and he could see immediately he looked a bit edgy, thinking, maybe, *what's going on here, something's not right, why's he being so friendly? He must hate my guts.*

Worried, are you? Notice I've got bigger? A bit of muscle on me now, eh?

All the time he was keeping the boy busy, he had a match burning in his hand, tucked up behind, just like a good soldier on night duty. When it had built up a good head, he dropped it into the boy's school bag as he turned to walk away.

He waited for the shouts. Just before he turned the corner, he saw the boy, bag on the pavement, trying to stamp out the flames.

People stopped and stared. He pissed himself laughing, and then stopped. Missed a trick there. Should've set his hair on fire. He'd do that the next time.

For the next few days, he expected a knock at the door. And another thrashing. He was used to thrashings by now. The knock didn't come. Not that time. The boy must have been too ashamed to admit what happened.

Taught you. I'll teach them all.

Not long after, his mother sent him to the shops again. This time, he pushed his luck. He'd got very good at forging signatures. He stole the chequebook out of the drawer where they kept it and wrote a cheque for cash. The shop owner, who knew his parents, wasn't about, so he persuaded the young guy at the till that his father had sent him because he was too busy to get away from the barber's shop. Too many customers. Needs to get off early. Third Tuesday in the month. Cobham Tuesday, see?

The young guy looked at him like he was a bit touched in the head. But he gave him the money all right. Scared not to, probably.

This time, the knock did come. And a thrashing, of course, worst yet. Still, he barely felt it now. He'd learned how not to.

All in the mind, you see.

The next decision was a surprise. They sent him away, to stay with his aunt and uncle. His mother's sister, a few years younger. He had no idea if he was ever going back. His parents explained nothing. No one did.

His aunt and uncle weren't much better. Well, in fairness, yes they were. Boring as fuck but at least they weren't brutal.

Still, didn't much matter where he stayed. He lived in his head most of the time now. It was better there.

With no warning, after a few weeks, months maybe, he couldn't tell, he was sent back.

His uncle dropped him off in the car, said a short goodbye and drove off.

He walked in, case in hand. His parents were standing waiting. Didn't say much, just 'go upstairs and unpack'.

When he came down, his mother told him his father wanted to see him in the garden. So he went out and there it was. A fence, ten foot high, all round.

'Do you see that?' his father asked.

He nodded. Couldn't bloody miss it, could he?

'No one will see you now. No one will find you. No one. Not even the Devil will find you here.'

He wasn't allowed out on his own anywhere for two years. He saw men in the shop, on Tuesdays and Saturdays, and the odd person on the way there and back, but that was it.

That's when he really started to lose it, he reckoned.

He'd sit on the swing for hours sometimes.

One hot summer's day, he was swinging back and forth. He started to think that, maybe, if he swung fast enough, high enough, he could fly right over the fence and be free.

He stopped swinging, stripped off his clothes, scattered them over the garden and ran around naked.

He got back on the swing and went faster and higher, the breeze licking his flesh all over, his legs apart, up in the air, wide open.

There you go my town, my world. My ass. Have a lick if you like.

He started laughing and couldn't stop. Swinging high and laughing like he was going to vomit on the whole world.

That's when he saw the man fall out of the aeroplane high up in the sky. The aeroplane went into a cloud and didn't come out the other side.

Just a dot at first, the man fell all the way down, soaring over the rooftops, drifting past the top of the fence, stopping for a moment to look at him. Who could he be? Not the Devil, because even the Devil couldn't find him here. An angel, then? Yes, an angel with a kind face, to catch him and carry him straight up to Heaven, for tea and cake, and no more tears.

Now it was clear. The plane was going to crash and everyone in it was on the way to Heaven.

He slowed down. He had this thought. This thought that in Heaven all you could do was stand still forever and ever and ever. Because that was the only way you could be good and never commit another sin. By not moving, not doing anything at all, like statues. He didn't much like the idea of that. It suffocated him, like he was paralysed and his mouth was filling with smoke and wax.

He decided he didn't want to go to Heaven after all. He just wanted to fly. So, he did. Straight through the air.

Go on, over the fence. You can do it.

He flipped over, landed on his back and hit his head on something sharp. He could feel the blood flowing, lovely and warm, like syrup, into the grass, the aeroplane still rising above him, the strength draining out of him.

Am I dying? Dying is nicer than I thought it would be. You can keep your Heaven. Give it to the statues. They deserve each other.

He closed his eyes.

When he opened them, he was in a hospital bed looking up at his father, his face a solid block of hate screwed tight into an angry red neck.

'You just won't be told, will you?'

When he got home, the swing was gone. His father had cut off the tyre and burned it in one corner of the garden. The rope was tied around the trunk of the tree, tight enough to spill sap and blood. Between the bark and the knot, the rabbit hung by its neck.

His father watched him from the window.

Shortly afterwards, the new lessons began.

Best seat in the house

It was disturbing. No doubt. He did look like Herman, the man standing, teeth bared in glee, spume in his chest hair, next to the enormous upended marlin, in the monochrome California sunshine of 1968. Only, at the same time, he did not look like him.

Jon wondered. Perhaps this was not an opportunity after all. Perhaps it was a mistake.

He had arrived ten minutes early for his 6.30 appointment with Dr Fisher. The practice was bright, neat and clean, with orange chairs in sculpted plastic, the soft light soothing against lime-green walls. Low but distinct, Andy Williams' 'Happy Heart' piped into the air, diffused on base notes of lavender and jasmine.

No one was waiting. Against one wall, a cream chaise longue invited him. Longing for sleep, he lay down and rested his head on the crisp linen cushion, spotted with patchouli and camomile.

'I'm so sorry,' the receptionist said, appearing, floating almost, from out of the shadows behind the counter. 'Dr Fisher has been called out on an emergency.'

How disappointing.

'I'm afraid that happens sometimes,' she said.

She wore a yellow-and-white polka-dot dress, green eye shadow and glossy pink lipstick. Her platinum hair piled itself high in a loose beehive. She said her name was Jean.

'Hi Jean.'

'Oh, they all make that joke.' She smiled, not knowing where to look, bashful as a beauty pageant.

'I wasn't making a joke.'

'Oh, they all say that too.'

'Do they?'

'Yes, but not sweet like you. Anyway, Dr Fisher asked me to register you and make another appointment.' She handed him the clipboard, forms and pen. 'Next week, same time, OK?'

'Yes, that should be fine.'

She smiled with all her teeth and told him to be sure and have a nice evening.

'Bye Jean.'

She floated back into the shadows behind the counter and out through a door at the back.

He found himself on the street, electric white flashing off the shattering London rain, a current running through the fillings in his teeth.

He looked up. There it was. The Green Lion, separated from Dr Fisher's practice by no more than the space of a panelled wooden door.

Perhaps not disappointing. Perhaps an opportunity.

The burnt-orange walls were covered with gilt-framed pictures spanning decades and continents, of actors and performers, military and political leaders, numerous fishing trips, and tribal peoples, huddled in trust, all smiles fixed for the explorer's lens.

One face looked out from every picture. It could only be him. Mercer.

The barman had been curious when Jon asked to see Mercer. Who was asking? Writer, actor, designer, dancer, producer? None of those. He stopped pouring a pint mid-flow, his face suddenly serious. Creditor? The bar went silent. Not that either, no. He continued pouring. Who then? Someone with a message from a friend. A good friend. Name? Herman. Herman? Yes, Herman. Herman who? A moment's thought. He'll know.

A mumbled telephone call and the barman, still suspicious, led Jon out to the street. He opened the panelled door and took him up a narrow stairwell to another door, top right.

'He'll be with you shortly. Have a seat.' The barman shut the door and left.

Beneath the photographs, dusty on a shelf, a stuffed bluebird sat on a perch in a cage.

Still no sign of the man himself.

The shelves were dense with books, bulging ring-bound

folders, a long metal box, a safety deposit box, perhaps, a moon-shaped silver hipflask, glinting bottles and coloured jars, full and half-full of coloured and clear liquids, and odd pieces of laboratory equipment – metal pipes, flasks, angle-brackets, a Bunsen burner and the like. A slightly nauseating smell that didn't belong, of gas, flame and chemicals, underlay the sweetness of books and the stonier odour of damp, which showed in patches on the walls.

A large wooden desk was covered in correspondence, bills, invoices, manila folders and dog-eared manuscripts. More manuscripts were piled high on the floor, on both sides.

A heavy step, a rattle of the handle and the door flew open. He blew into the room, a plate balanced perfectly on his fingertips.

Mercer. Without doubt, Mercer.

He registered Jon as he swept around the desk, landing on his chair.

He wore pale-green corduroy trousers, a mustard corduroy jacket with leather elbow patches, a blue jumper and a white shirt with red stripes, the collar worn at the points. His grey hair was plastered to his skull like a bush fire under control.

He set about his meal of artichoke, salad and lemon. With mouth full, he nodded towards the chair on the other side of the desk.

Jon sat down.

Mercer pushed the barely touched meal into the middle of the desk.

'What can I do for you?' Mercer asked, the thinnest trace

of an American accent detectable under layers of English and European emulsion.

'Herman told me about you,' Jon said.

'Herman?'

'You met him in Prague. He's written a play. He told me what you can do.'

'The big fat German man-baby? The Bavarian?'

'Prussian, I think.'

'Prussian, you say. My, my. I thought he was called Piers.'

'Do you mean Peirce?'

'Was it Peirce? No matter.' Mercer clicked his tongue hard against one cheek, the focus in his eyes suggesting that all synapses were firing smoothly, as he made an initial, and possibly final, assessment. 'What exactly did this Prussian tell you?'

Jon told him, as best he could remember.

'Not exactly how I remember it.'

'Is his play any good?'

'Not yet. Needs work. Not sure he gets that.'

'So, do you like it at all?'

'I think I like the title.'

'What is the title?'

'Haven't a clue. Why are we talking about him?' Mercer asked, reaching behind him and grabbing a bottle of cloudy liquid and two glasses off the lowest shelf. 'Drink?'

'If you're not too busy.'

'I have creditors to fend off and books to cook that are already stewed. Happy to make an excuse of you,' Mercer said, filling two glasses.

The slightly bitter aftertaste, of fungus or wet wood, something rotten, was less sickening than before, and the drink took effect much more quickly.

'What is this stuff?' Jon asked.

'You look to me,' Mercer said, 'like a man with an open mind, yes?'

'Some would say open wide.'

Mercer sniffed. 'I graduated in chemistry, in the early sixties. In the right place at the right time.'

'To do what?'

'To help those in power control.'

'Control what?'

'The supply of LSD and other drugs. Before I knew it, I was a highly prized intelligence resource, a spy, an arms trader, an agent provocateur, a drug dealer, the Santa Claus of psychedelia, the witch doctor of western intelligence. Militarily, morally, politically – in fact, in every way that mattered, and many more that didn't, I was a double agent. I was so schizoid for the best part of two decades that even I didn't always know, how can I put it—?'

'Whose side you were on?'

'It wasn't my job to take sides. It was my job to play all sides, to be all sides. To foment unrest, wherever it was needed, and then monitor it, direct it, play it, betray it and provide it with its drug of choice. And if it didn't have one, it was my job also to make sure it chose one, and quickly. I got to travel the world, party with indigenous peoples and do some serious cooking.'

'Cooking?'

'Ergot, ayahuasca, peyote and ololiuqui, chewed pituri, yagé, the telepathic vine, the fly agaric mushroom, cannabis, LSD, mescaline and a whole lot more you won't find in the textbooks. I analysed, I improvised, I refined. I was the spooks' cook and everybody wanted a seat at the table.'

'You make drugs.'

'Psychedelics. My friends in Europe knew nothing about my associates in Africa, and those in Asia hadn't a clue what I got up to back home. I ran a tight operation in France, and had plans to turn on the Soviets, the Chinese and the Japanese. I had a cosy number in Florence, and a fondness for the classier hotels of Rome, Milan and Venice. In '74, I had to abandon a lab in Bologna in a hurry when my partner made off with the cash, the kitchen and the last 100 grams of LSD. He had debts. He hanged himself.'

'Sounds tragic.'

'It happens.' Mercer shrugged, refilling their glasses. 'I helped tear Paris apart in '68, basked in the hot autumn of Milan in '69 and carpet-bombed the California Bay Area with hallucinogens in the early seventies. Things came to an inglorious end in Prague a few years later. Had to sweat it out for a while in prison but my connections came through.'

'Connections?'

'I knew where the bodies were buried. I knew about those in the morgue. And more that could find their way there, quickly enough, if necessary. I had a pocket full of toe-tags. Still, it was bye-bye Prague. Had to wait until the velvet revolution – my favourite kind – before I could set foot there again.'

'Now you run a shabby theatre. At the back of a pub. In a nondescript London street. Why?'

'I kept my finances liquid,' Mercer said, nodding towards the long metal box on the shelf. 'I had to earn somehow. I'd always had an eye for art. A few careful investments here and there paid off. By natural extension, art led me to theatre. Amusement level high, profile low, hidden in plain sight. Still, theatre's not what it was. If things don't pick up, I'll be pulling the plug real soon.'

The extravagant implausibility tortured into coherence. Delusion snapping at the heels of reason. He resisted. Yet, it seduced.

Mercer gave him a wide, knowing look.

Jon shot to his feet. Mercer, with a firm upward flip, sent the sash window rattling upwards. Jon was just in time to heave a clatter of vomit into the alley below.

He fell back onto his seat, wiping porridge-brown puke on his cuff.

Mercer grinned, got up and grabbed a bottle of pure, clear liquid and two fresh glasses. He set them on the desk and sat down again.

'What's this?' Jon asked.

'My finest work,' Mercer said. 'The best seat in the house, the hottest ticket, the only show in town your neurotransmitters have ever wanted to see. Now, tell me, why did Herman send you to me?'

'He said you gave him another life.'

'Did he now?' Mercer filled both glasses, pushing one towards Jon.

Jon lifted his glass.

'Not yet,' Mercer said. 'Not so hasty.'

'Sorry.' Jon set down his glass.

'So, you think I can offer you one too?'

'Can you?'

'What's wrong with the one you have?'

'It doesn't work.'

'In what way doesn't it?'

'I'm broken. I was made wrong.'

'You weren't made wrong,' Mercer said. 'You were made unmade, unfinished. Everyone is. Little more than salt, pepper and roots tossed into a bowl. Still, at least you're aware of that – that's a start. It never occurs to most people. But what makes you think that another life will be any better?'

'I'm out of options,' Jon said. 'And I have a very bad feeling about where this one is heading.'

'And where is that, exactly?'

'Towards some terrible rupture.'

'Why?'

'Because I am full of rage and hate.'

'Anything else?'

'I am in possession of profound harm that does not belong to me. I would like to return it to its owner.'

'Is that everything?'

'No.'

'What else?'

'Love does not belong to me.'

'Why not?'

'Because I am wrong. Badly made, the worst.'

'You are unmade, that is all,' Mercer corrected. 'Unbecome.'

'Can you fix that?'

'Do you think I can?'

'Yes.'

'Why? Because of what Herman told you? Why believe him?'

'I know that he is both dead and alive, yet more alive than dead, and that you have something to do with that.'

'I'm not sure this is right for you.'

'Why not?'

'Because you haven't told me what you actually want?'

'I want to see how I am unmade.'

'And if you don't get to see that? What then?'

'Then this life will end badly.'

Mercer nodded and pointed at the glass. 'Down the hatch.'

Jon knocked it back in one, and Mercer did the same.

The room went black. For a long time, maybe no time, nothing happened. The room then lit up with colours before turning white, then red. The red swelled and became the space all around him, a formless, unclaimed cathedral, a magnificence of absence.

Some way off, he saw a pulsing light, orbited by smaller lights. He focused and they came closer, passing through him, and he through them, into a mesh of possibilities – a place, not a place, of waves that were points, and points that were waves, and each made of neither, and of both, and all of it made of nothing at all.

He saw and passed into the seed that projected life in all directions, lives to which he was forever connected. He saw himself, young, old, male and female. Cutting hedges on suburban Sundays. Cut to pieces in foreign fields. Cut to fit every shape, every variation on a theme.

He remembered now that he had forgotten everything. That he had remembered everything, and forgotten again. Remembered, forgotten. Countless times.

He came to understand that his life, these lives, without ever fully knowing why or how, endlessly rebalanced the distribution of grace and debt. They drew at the deepest level from a pool of experience known to all of them, even the dead, who, forever transiting the space between lives, were also always alive.

And behind, in and under all was love. He did not just come to know this. He inhabited it. He became it. For just a second, if it could be called that, he rose above everything and saw beauty and suffering resolve in perfect mathematics, then separate and dissolve, eating and regurgitating each other in an endless loop.

He looked down and then he fell.

He felt a shadow cast over him and a roaring sound split his eardrums. He rotated, looked up and saw an aeroplane just a few feet above him. The livery said Pan-American. Someone was waving at him from a cabin window. It was Jean in all her Technicolor tenderness.

'Hi Jean,' he mouthed.

'Oh, they all make that joke,' she smiled, all teeth and platinum.

'I wasn't making a joke,' he mouthed back.

She just gazed at him, happy and sad.

He twisted around and continued his fall.

Below, he saw a tight grid of buildings and houses. He soared over them, descending, floating past a high fence.

The naked boy on the swing looked him in the eye, revealing the map of his unmaking, like a nervous system unfurled, splayed and nailed to a table.

He remembered he had fallen many times. Falling now, he fell each time again, and fell too all those times he had not yet fallen.

He drifted on past the fence.

'Do any of them recognise you?' Mercer asked.

'Some,' Jon said. 'One in particular.'

'Where is he?'

'He's sitting at a table, with his back to me.'

'What is he doing?'

'He's talking to someone. He senses me behind him. I am trying to speak to him but he cannot hear me above the noise. He wants to turn, but cannot. He has no doubt though that I am there.'

'Does he welcome you?'

'He wants, more than anything, for things to be made clear,' Jon said. 'He is finally reaching a decision that has been a long time coming. How different everything will be tomorrow, he thinks. How surprised they will be when they read the letter – twenty pages, tightly written.'

'But does he welcome you?' Mercer asked again.

'Yes, I think he does.'

'Is he amenable?'

'Yes, I think he is.'

'Enough,' Mercer said, slapping the desk.

Jon tried to hold the scene in his mind but it dissolved and was gone. He sat silent, bliss reluctantly deferring to measurable time.

'Good show?' Mercer asked.

Jon took slow, deep breaths.

Mercer stood up, reached for the moon-shaped silver flask on the shelf, unscrewed the stopper and filled it from the bottle.

'What's this now?' Jon asked.

'One for the road,' Mercer said, pushing the stopper back in and handing him the flask. 'Take it.'

Jon took it.

'Good.' Mercer rubbed his hands together, brisk and business like, eyeing the papers on his desk. 'OK, I'll call you then.'

'When?'

'When it's time to make the exchange,' Mercer said. 'And not before. Is that clear?'

'Yes.'

'Excellent. Well, that's all for now. Dallying is always an exquisite guilty pleasure, but this place can't run itself into the ground without me. So, go home, get some rest and carry on with life as normal.'

Jon nodded, feeling time settle back into itself, every second heavy with the disappointment of seeing itself again.

'Now, you know your way out, don't you?'

The Devil's teardrops

His father set the Bible, his belt, a notebook and a pen on top of the piano. He then sat on the stool at the piano and told him to sit on the hard chair facing him. He could see the beads of sweat on the old man's brow, his greasy hair, prematurely silver, hanging over the right side of his face, dripping into his eye. He pushed it back, revealing his hard grey-blue eyes. To show how determined he was, how much this mattered, do you see?

His father did a reading from the Bible and asked him to recite it back to him, just as he'd read it. He made him repeat it over and over until he got it word perfect and then asked him what he thought the reading meant.

He had a stab at saying something, but he knew his father didn't really care what he thought. He was just waiting for him to finish, so he could tell him what it meant.

The following Sunday and the one after, it was the same routine.

On the fourth Sunday, after his father had done his reading and gone through the usual farce, he asked him to give him a summary of the reading from the first week and tell him what it meant. In other words, repeat back to him, word for word, from memory, what he'd said it meant.

He wasn't expecting that. He didn't have a clue. Couldn't remember a thing.

'Nothing?' his father asked.

He shook his head.

'I see,' his father said, offering him the pen and notebook. 'Perhaps you might find it easier to write it down.'

He stared at the notebook and pen. Ah, leaving them on the piano from week one was supposed to be a clue. That's how his father's mind worked, do you see?

His father stabbed with the pen at the open blank page, leaving small black dashes.

'No ideas?'

'No,' he said, staring at the page, the black marks wriggling like tiny worms of hate.

'Strip,' his father said.

He stood in front of him, naked again, hands by his side. It was cold in that room, always. For a long time, well it seemed like a long time, his father said nothing, just stared at him. If he dared to meet his father's gaze, he told him not to. So he looked past him, focusing on the light reflecting off the polished wood of the piano lid.

The clock ticking on the wall melted into the sounds of washing-up from the kitchen, along with the smells of beef, vegetables, grease and soapsuds. The light in the wood of the piano cut right to the back of his eyes. His head was light. Colours turned electric. He felt like the room was upside down, that he was going to fall from the floor to the ceiling. The wriggling worms of hate spilled from the blank page onto the carpet and multiplied. He dug in his toes, just to hold on. The worms crawled over his feet and up his ankles.

He didn't know why, but his cock just started to rise. Sprang up like it was pointing straight at his father, in accusation, hard as a rock.

His father pointed a finger back at it, his face screwed up in disgust.

He looked down and saw a teardrop form in the eye of his cock. He could smell himself now. The pearls of being, like bleach, or something like, now added to the mix of beef, vegetables, soapsuds, pots and pans banging, and time ticking, every second measurable. His breath thinned to a white whistle, piercing the ceiling, rising up into the sky, dissolving into contrails, begging release from flesh and time.

'You have the Devil's teardrops in you,' his father said. 'Do you know why the Devil cries? To make us pity him so that we offer him shelter in the house of our flesh, to trick us into begetting his filthy bastards, propagating ruin and stealing everything that is rightfully the Lord's.'

He swayed from side to side.

'Come here,' his father said. 'Come here that I might

empty out his dirty water. Like a doctor drains a wound of infection. And then you'll be clean, and the Lord can take you into the corpus eternal without wanting to vomit you out of his mouth at the very sight of you.'

On behalf of the Lord, and maybe the Devil, his father tugged away.

After the Devil had shed his tears, his father thrashed him again, dead-eyed, relentless. When he'd done, he told him to get dressed and sent him to his room to study.

So it continued every Sunday, after lunch.

Once, his mother walked in on them. Easily done, as his father never locked the door. It didn't even have a lock. His father didn't feel the need. That said it all, really. That particular Sunday, his father hadn't yet got down to the actual business. All the same, no mistaking what was going on.

What is she going to do? Surely she'll do something.

But she didn't. Well, she had a look. A good, long look, she had. Then she looked at his father, a very different kind of look. The old man knew she was there but he didn't even bother to turn round. Just waited for her to shut the door so he could carry on. So she did. And so did he.

Later, after his father was dead and buried, she used to say, 'I always loved you, you know. I never wanted you to come to any harm. I couldn't stop him.'

Who was she trying to convince? Just what did she want? What exactly did she think she deserved? Forgiveness? Absolution? No, much worse. Pity.

Bill looked Jack in the eye and pushed his empty glass across the table. 'Pity? From me? Bit rich, don't you think?'

'So, it was her fault?' Jack asked.

'It was her look. And a look is all it takes.'

'To do what?'

'Destroy someone.'

'So you do blame her?'

'I blame the drink. Speaking of which—' Bill tapped his glass on the table.

'So, you do blame her.'

'Yes.'

'Why?'

'She should've stopped him.'

'How?'

'However the fuck she liked. Who else could?'

'You say he died?'

'Yeah, long time ago now.'

'How?'

'Died at work.'

'And is she still alive?'

'Rumour has it, and medical science insists it's true, so I guess between the two we must agree that she is. But you know what they say, never listen to rumours. Or doctors.'

'Indeed,' Jack said, getting up. 'Nature calls.'

As Jack's foot hit the stair, Bill got up and searched the pockets of Jack's leather waistcoat. In the right-hand pocket, he found the wallet Jack had taken from him. He put it back. In the left-hand pocket, he found Jack's wallet. He slipped it, without opening it, into his own back pocket and sat down again.

Jack came back down.

'Tell me about the accident,' he said, sitting down.

'What accident?' Bill gave his glass a firm tap.

'Your father's death.'

'Never said anything about any accident.' He grinned.

Jack lifted the bottle.

Table for three

The waiter nodded politely to the group of four at the table next to Jon and turned sharply on his heel, giving him a short ,searching look as he headed towards the bar.

Jon drummed his fingers.

So, let me see. Tonight we have Adam and Lisa, Helen and Jez. Is that right? Not left anyone out, have I? No. Excellent.

The group toasted Helen and Jez's engagement, the lucky couple interleaving, then loosening, their fingers as they kissed and sipped champagne.

All four gave him a look and eyed each other. Lisa coughed.

Am I staring? Do I care? You don't own the place.

'Jez, I'm just…' Helen said, getting up.

'Of course,' Jez said, shooting him another look, his fingers fidgeting with the stem of his glass.

Helen returned.

Back so soon? Aren't you dainty?

'More champagne here.' Adam clicked his fingers.

'The same?' the waiter asked.

'The same,' Adam ordered, in a flat, clotted bark, dispatching shards of mucus to the chamber of his chest.

Oh, Adam, what have you been doing? Smoking like a squaddie in wartime? Twenty years minimum, I'd say. Did the corporate fear get to you? Dear me. Heart attack on the cards for you, I'd say. Or cancer. Two dogs. One rabbit. Only one way that race ends, Adam.

Only one way it ever ends.

The waiter turned to Jon.

'And are you ready to order yet?'

He didn't answer. Seemed unaware the waiter had even spoken.

'Congratulations,' Adam said again.

Yes, fucking congratulations all round.

The waiter was waiting for an answer.

Helen, Jez, Lisa and Adam fell silent.

Seems I'm staring. How very rude of me.

'Sir?' the waiter asked.

'What—?' Jon glanced at the empty chair. 'I'm still waiting for—'

Mark arrived.

'Oh, here he is,' Jon said.

The waiter looked relieved, though not much.

'Another bottle of the white, please. We'll order food shortly,' Jon said, scratching the back of his head.

The waiter grimaced and left.

'Hi,' Mark said, settling himself.

'Hi. I'm glad you came.'

'I said I would.'

Weeks had gone by and Jon had heard nothing from Mercer. Weeks in which Jon had felt better than he had for a long time. One evening, he picked up the phone. He was surprised that Mark answered. Mark was surprised too. What did he want? To apologise, make amends, clear the air. There was a long silence.

'Dinner, on me,' Jon said.

'Really no need,' Mark said.

'Please. It shouldn't have ended that way.'

True, they agreed.

'Tomorrow, at eight?'

A moment's thought and a few more in negotiation.

'OK,' Mark relented. 'Tomorrow at eight.'

The waiter beetled back to their table and took their order. Mark wasted no time in placing his, and it wasn't much. He wasn't drinking, Jon noticed.

They ate, largely in silence, getting it out of the way as quickly as they could. With plates empty, they faced each other.

'Anything else?' the waiter asked.

'No, thanks,' Mark said.

'No, thank you,' Jon said.

'Coffee?' asked the waiter.

Jon looked at Mark. He reconsidered.

'Filtered, black. Thanks.'

'The same,' Jon said.

The waiter scurried off again.

'So, thing is—' Mark said.

'The thing is,' Jon said, 'that I need to tell you how sorry I am. You deserve that. And I need you to know that I mean it, more than I've ever meant anything. I regret what I said and did that night more than anything I've ever done. I have no excuse.'

'You were off your—'

'No excuse,' Jon insisted. 'I need you to forgive me. But if you can't forgive me – and I'll understand if you can't – then I just need you to believe that I am sorry, really, truly sorry.'

'I do believe you,' Mark said.

'Can you forgive me?'

'I forgive you. I know you're not well and anyway—'

'I'll take the pills. I'll go to the doctors. I'll do whatever it takes.'

Mark's face sagged onto his hands like wet clay.

'Whatever it takes,' Jon repeated.

'Whatever it takes for what?'

Jon's face said it all.

'No,' Mark said. 'I forgive you, but we, no, that's not happening. Not ever.'

'You can fix me.'

'I can't fix you.'

'You can make me.'

'Make you?'

'I'm unmade.'

'Unmade?'

'Yes, unmade, but with you, I can be made,' Jon said. 'With you, if you're with me—'

'You're doing it again.'

'Doing what?'

'Mistaking love for therapy.'

'I'm sorry.'

'Please stop apologising.'

'Can't we—?'

'Jon, you're just not…'

'What?'

'You're just not boring enough for me.'

Mark's mobile rang. He answered it. 'Hi, yes, probably a bit longer. Not sure. No, don't. Don't do that. Don't— Fuck.' He slipped the phone back into his pocket.

'Who was that?'

'Doesn't matter,' Mark said. 'Listen, we should get the bill.'

'Don't you have anything more to say?'

'Not really.'

Jon's face fell.

'Not here, not now,' Mark said, softer, scribbling a line in the air for the waiter, who was suddenly very busy.

'I need the loo,' Jon said.

'I'll get the bill,' Mark said.

'No, I'm paying.'

'It doesn't matter.'

'It does matter. I'm paying. I said I would.'

Mark surrendered.

Jon left the table.

He stood over the basin. He felt sick. Whatever it takes? What did that mean? He hadn't planned that. He hadn't planned anything at all. He felt sicker.

Returning to the table, Jon saw another man in his seat, with his back to him. As he got closer, Jon sensed that the man wanted to turn but could not. Sensed that he was about to make a decision that had been a long time coming.

Jon stopped. There was also another man sitting next to Mark.

He found himself in his chair again.

'Hello Jon,' said the man next to Mark.

'Hello Matt,' Jon said.

'How are you? Haven't seen you in a while.' Matt reached to take Mark's hand in his, squeezing it tight between Mark's legs in a clear declaration of ownership.

A blade slid the full length of Jon's gut, twisted and sliced back on itself.

Mark pulled his hand free, gently pushed Matt's away and looked at Jon as if to say – at least now you know.

The waiter arrived with the bill.

'How's Nick?' Jon asked.

'Oh, you know,' Matt said with a grin, 'moved on, as people do.'

'So I see.'

Does he never stop grinning?

Jon offered his card to the waiter, and all the way from the kitchen he heard a plate fall and shatter.

The waiter went to take the card.

Jon held it tight as the room raced towards him, then from him.

'Sir?'

He let go of the card.

The other man, the man he sensed, the one who so badly needed to make a decision, and finally act, was now joined to him, brain stem to brain stem, looking over the same restaurant, which was, at the same time, not the same restaurant. He strained to turn, to rip and tear, to look at Jon, eye to eye, and acknowledge him so that Jon could finally accept. That love did not belong to him. Hate belonged to him. Hate was his. He had not been wrong to hate. He had simply hated imperfectly. He had not seen it through to its logical conclusion. In that moment, Jon knew the other man and, at last, stopped resisting and became exactly what he was – a thing made of jealousy, rage and hate.

He signed the slip of paper and dropped some coins, more than were needed, onto the shiny metal tip dish. The waiter scraped them gracelessly into his hand.

The edge of a coin caught the candlelight, forming a splinter that pierced Jon's eye. It entered his brain, spreading out, netting it in a diffuse wave, gathering data, before collapsing into a frequency that encoded the true and complete nature of his want, and the precise sequence of its repeated and inevitable failure. It then directed itself, in unstoppable trajectory, straight at Matt's rattling bucket of a head. It drilled into his forehead and ripped out through the back of his skull, struck the far window and ricocheted around the room, triggering heated collisions within the glass, the plaster, the metal, the walls, the wood, boiling even the molecules of the air, escalating everything towards some savage rupture.

'Are you alright?' Mark asked Jon.

He is not deep inside me at all. I am.

'Is he having a fit?' Matt whispered.

Jon's mobile rang. He answered it.

'Is that you?' Mercer asked.

'Yes, it's me,' Jon said.

'It's time to make the exchange.'

'Of course it is,' Jon said, hitting the off-button. 'Now then, who's for a drink? My place.'

Mark and Matt looked at each other.

'I'm not sure,' Mark said.

'Why not?' Matt asked. 'I've never seen your place. Can't wait to see what you've done with it.'

He will stop grinning.

'Not tonight,' Mark said.

'Just one drink,' Jon said, the moon-shaped silver flask glinting on the shelf in his mind's eye. 'To show there are no hard feelings. We all move on.'

'Great,' Matt said.

Grinning is the last thing he'll do.

'Definitely just the one,' Jon said, beaming at them both. He didn't lie.

Seventeen minutes

He settled on the third Tuesday in November. He had seventeen minutes. He'd timed it on his way home, most Tuesdays and Saturdays since summer. He'd counted precisely the minutes between the light in the shop bathroom upstairs going off and the one downstairs going off, as his father left by the front door for the drive to Cobham to 'do the books'. Or fuck the other woman, to give things their proper name.

Did his mother know? Probably. Certainly, other people did. That's how he found out. His father could lock him up all he liked. But gossip, like water, will always find a crack.

On those days he didn't linger in the back alley, he practised building an extra seventeen minutes into his walk home, perfecting the long route, so that when the day came, he'd be back at his usual time, nothing out of the ordinary.

He had seventeen minutes to leave by the front door, walk down the High Street just beyond the bend, nip down a covered side alley, dart back up through the backstreets, with his head down, keeping to the shadows – never many people about anyway, he'd checked – and let himself in, quietly, through the back door with the key the cat had knocked off the wall.

He'd then have thirteen minutes. Two minutes to make sure the front door was locked and the blinds rolled down. To strip naked, pile his clothes neatly on the small stool in the corner, well out of the way, and slip on the yellow rubber gloves, kept with the brushes and detergents in the grey bucket under the sink.

Under a minute to lift the soap dispenser out of its cradle, both screws already loosened in preparation, turn off the downstairs light and hunker down behind the curve of the banister, just under the light switches.

The bathroom door would open. He would then have a little bit less than ten minutes. His father would see the place in darkness below. But he wouldn't necessarily think much of it. Most likely the bulb, he'd think. Happened all the time, burning in the shop all day long, old wiring and all that. He'd flick on the stair light, walk straight down and come round the curve of the banister to try the switch. Because he always tried the switch, just to see, as you would, before searching for a new bulb, in the cupboard under the stair, where the spares were kept.

He would have just a few seconds before his father put his foot on the last step, ready to turn. He would have to time it precisely. Reach up to turn off the stair light and stretch to full height, without making a sound, the heavy soap dispenser tightly gripped in the cup of both hands.

The stair light going off would stop his father in his tracks. He'd pause for a second on the step and look back up the stairs before stepping onto the shop floor. That would be his moment.

One blow, that was all he'd need. More would be nice – to take his time, really enjoy it, but one blow was all he had time for. He knew his father's height and frame. And he'd had plenty of practice in the dark.

In that darkness, he would drag his father across the shop and dump him in the barber's chair. He'd take the jack-knife razor off its hook, open it and hold it in his right hand. He'd stand to one side, legs apart, firm on his feet, grip his father by the scalp with his left hand, pull his head back, just enough so his throat was still well over the basin, reach in and slit it, just once, clean from side to side.

So far, bang on schedule.

He had about seven minutes left. As the blood poured onto the white porcelain, like ice-cream sauce, his father jerked in his grip, frantic, bug-eyed, a thick gurgling in his throat. He took a moment to relish the thought of his father's nerves in electric convulsion, and adrenalin pumping hard enough to pop his eyes out of their sockets and, maybe just, on a good day, struggle free.

But this was not that day.

'You're dying, do you see? You relentless cunt.' He held his father's head back, just far enough, just long enough, for him to see himself in the mirror.

Then, he smashed his head, just once, off the tiles above the basin. Well, twice for good measure.

'Got a bit of muscle on me now. Hadn't you noticed?'

His father jerked again, so he smashed his head again.

There, now. That's that little hitch taken care of.

The blood ran down the plughole and his father's body went limp. He pulled his corpse in and up at the waist, forcing his back into more of an arch to make sure the basin fully supported his head and neck, his knees jammed firmly under.

There, steady now. Won't matter if you fall off later.

He rinsed the gloves under the tap and left them on the draining board. He unwrapped a new pair and put them in the bucket under the sink.

Five minutes, give or take.

He shot upstairs, still in darkness, and examined his naked body in the bathroom mirror, by the strip light only.

Not bad at all. Quite neat, in fact. A few splashes here and there.

He rinsed himself off in the shower, in less than a minute, and examined himself again.

Clean. Job well done.

Downstairs, he dressed, tiptoed across the shop floor, around his father's body, its head still in the basin, and quietly unlocked the front door. He wrapped the gloves in paper towels and put them in his right coat pocket. He emptied the cash register, stuffing the money into his inside pocket, and left by the back door, locking it after him.

He took a breath, hunkered by the bins and checked both directions. Lights on, muffled TVs, curtains drawn, steamed windows, cabbage and bacon cooking, but no one about. He kept to the shadows, down the backstreets, head down, and nipped into the covered side alley. Another quick check, both directions: two women and a child on one side; a man on the other.

Give it a minute and, yes, they're out of sight.

He slipped unnoticed back onto the path just beyond the bend in the High Street and continued on his normal route home. A minute to spare, he reckoned, so he slowed his pace. No need to rush.

Home on time, he was. Nothing out of the ordinary. Not at all.

'Your father doing the books?'

'Yes.'

'Ready for tea?'

'In a minute,' he said. 'Just going up to change.'

She nodded and stirred something grey in a pot. He and his mother had permission to eat alone on Cobham Tuesdays, as his father wouldn't get home until late, usually about nine.

He lifted a corner of the carpet in his room and flipped up the loose floorboard beneath. He placed the rubber gloves, the money and the key in the hiding place he'd used since they'd discovered the box in the drawer. As he patted the carpet back into place, the happy thought occurred to him that he'd never have to work in the shop again.

He thought about having a wank. He was so in the mood for a good long, hard one. Best not, he decided. Save it for later.

His father wasn't more than half an hour late before his mother began to wonder. By ten, she already looked tense. Not long after, she was on the phone. To the shop, her sister, the police, in that order.

It was the police who found him, on the floor. Bound to happen. Handy, as it turned out. Caused more of a mess. That, and the empty cash register, pointed to a robbery gone wrong, with resulting violence, though not everyone was convinced. The slit throat raised questions. He was relieved, though, that he hadn't had time to enjoy it as much as he wanted to. That, he discovered later, would have pointed to a crime of hate, and that would have raised even more questions.

He was quite proud of that, to tell you the truth. He'd had the right instincts. Did a professional job. His father would surely have approved.

Good thing too that he saved the pleasure for later, for when he was alone. Lying in the dark, the memory of his father's face in the mirror.

That's it. Make sure he knows he no longer has the power. Don't leave any doubt. Then punch the face. Keep punching it. And when the eyes tell you that he really can't take any more, punch it again. Again and again and again.

Sleep. Wake again. Hate again.

Anyway, as it was, his story stood up. He played it shocked

166

and confused. A bit simple, even. Mouth hanging open. Just a bit. Nice touch.

His mother confirmed he was home on time and that his father had the only set of keys. No one, it turned out, recalled seeing him on the High Street or in the backstreets, at any time. Ever.

Of course, his mother never said anything about what went on in the home. She knew not to. Think of the trouble she'd have been in then. Jail, maybe, for never having stopped it. Scandal and shame, certainly. They agreed that much in a look, even as the police were on their way.

Yes, officers, it was usual for her husband to be home late on the third Tuesday of each month. That's when he did the books, you see.

That, too, led to questions and, quick enough, it all came out about the woman in Cobham.

More questions, murk, malicious gossip and confusion, all happily pointing away from him, towards some unimaginably evil person. He enjoyed every opportunity to stare into people's pitying eyes.

Fingers pointed at his mother for a bit, but those dots wouldn't be joined either. Then towards the husband of the woman in Cobham, who very soon after stopped working unsociable hours. Nothing clicked there either, of course, but it was distracting, and therefore useful while it lasted.

In fact, in time, despite a great deal of effort, nothing stuck to anyone at all. Unsolved, his father's murder simply became a permanent mysterious stain on the town.

He wasted little time, and chose his moment well, after things had died down. He threw the gloves and the money in the river one night. He'd been tempted to spend it but no, best not, he decided. He buried the key on the heath, at the spot where he and Benny got drunk on cider, talked about girls and looked at the stars.

He was sent back to school. Had a lot of catching up to do. He stayed only as long as he had to. Left with some qualifications, not many, a handful, just enough to separate him from the animals. As far as he could make out.

He could meet girls now. He could do what he wanted. His mother didn't try to stop him, didn't dare. He met a girl he liked. Well, he met a few, but he liked this one in particular.

What was it she was called? No good, the name's gone. Won't come back. Definitely pretty though.

Anyway, one night, he took her to the heath and fucked her on the spot he'd buried the key. As he was doing it, he thought how perfect it would be if Benny were there to watch. But Benny, so he'd heard, had gone to London in search of a man.

Never mind. Can't have everything.

After he came, he ground into her even harder, like he wanted to come right through her. Shoot his sticky load into the soil, so it could glue itself to the key and seed death in the ground. He imagined an embryo of death, his father's death, all death, two-headed, butting the dark, desperate to chew its way out of the dirt with its tiny misshapen teeth.

He heard a noise and looked down.

She was crying, pleading for him to stop. He did. He'd nothing against her. Nice enough girl. He'd just lost himself there for a minute.

Others would cry too. Of course, sometimes, that's exactly what he wanted. Other times, he just had to shut them up.

Not long after, she told him, half hopeful, half-crying in her drink, that she was pregnant.

'Shall I keep it? Do you want it? Do you want me?'

'Of course I do,' he said. 'Don't cry. It'll work out, you'll see.'

He joined up a few days later and never saw her again.

'Bosnia?' His mother sat at the kitchen table, grey, small, a yellow handkerchief screwed up in her knotted hand. She cried now, all the time. Hadn't stopped since the funeral. He hated her for that more than for everything she hadn't done before.

'Yes,' he said. 'Bosnia.'

'When?'

'Tomorrow.'

'Tomorrow? So soon? Why didn't you tell me?'

He shrugged and went upstairs to pack.

He set his last bag, the big one, by the front door, opened it and pulled on his jacket.

'Taxi will be here in a minute,' he said.

She stood in the hallway, twisting her handkerchief.

'I think that's him,' he said, gathering up his bags. 'He's just making the turn.'

'Was it you?' she asked.

Outside, the driver beeped his horn.

169

'That's me,' he said.

'Was it?'

Another beep.

'Yeah, it was me. Course it was.'

She looked like she might fall over, punched by a fist she'd seen coming for years.

Seriously, though. Who the fuck was she kidding?

'Bye Jean,' he said, turning, pushing the door wide open with one knee, struggling out with his bags, dropping them onto the step. 'Take care of yourself. Find someone else. It's not too late.'

With those words, she was no longer his mother.

The taxi driver got out, opened the boot and came up the path to help him.

'Thanks mate.'

He closed the door behind him.

That yellow paint could do with touching up.

You don't live there anymore

Jon opened his eyes. A small detonation had gone off in his head, or so it seemed, leaving a ragged hole into which some animal had crawled as he slept. Terrified, it clawed at the back of his eyes, digging deeper into his brain.

'Time to get up,' Mercer said.

Jon lay on a narrow single bed, pressed tight into a corner, with a hard mattress, one flat pillow and a plain, grey blanket. It was a small room, more of a cell, with unpainted plaster walls. To his left, on the other side of the room, were a cheap chest of drawers and a wardrobe. Next to a bedside table with his wallet on it, there was a small wash basin with a glass tumbler, a toothbrush, toothpaste, razors and a fresh can of shaving foam. Next to it was a toilet and, squeezed into the opposite corner, behind a cheap plastic curtain, a shower. A small hand towel and a thin bath towel hung on simple hooks in the wall. Up above, the open skylight allowed in a fixed meanness of air.

Between the end of the bed and the far wall, Mercer sat on a hard, wooden chair by a small desk. He got up and set a glass of orange juice on the bedside table.

'Drink this,' he said. 'The sugar will help.'

Jon sat up, put his feet to the floor and drank the juice.

'Do you remember?' he asked.

'Remember what?'

Mercer took a rolled-up newspaper out of his pocket and handed it to Jon, pointing to one particular story. The headline ran: 'Two dead in Angel knife slaying'.

Jon read the details of how two men in their thirties, subsequently identified as Mark Fludd and Matt Stevens, had been murdered in a flat close to the Angel. The precise details of how they died were not given. From the evidence contained in a twenty-page letter of tightly scribbled lines found at the scene, the police, the item went on to say, 'had good reason to believe that the killer was the occupant of the flat, Jon Young, 35, who had not been seen or heard from since'.

A forensic psychiatrist said that 'the content of the letter, evidence at the scene, the handwriting and the frenzied nature of the attack all suggested a disorganised killer, probably a paranoid schizophrenic'. The police confirmed reports that 'Mr Young had a long history of serious mental illness, including numerous psychotic episodes'. They were appealing for witnesses or 'anyone with knowledge of Mr Young's whereabouts to come forward'. They also warned that 'he' was 'a serious danger to both himself and members of the public and should not be approached'. A bad portrait picture accompanied the piece.

Jon set the newspaper on the bedside table.

'I did this?' he asked.

'Yes,' Mercer said. 'You don't remember?'

'No.'

'You will. Eventually all the details will come back to you and there will be no denying it.'

'I did this last night?'

'Look at the date,' Mercer said, pointing at the newspaper's front page.

Jon looked at it. 'So?'

Mercer pulled a rolled-up magazine out of his pocket and pointed at its date. Apparently, weeks had passed.

'So, I…?'

'Yes, you did it weeks ago. We've been hiding you. At first, in a remote place and then, when it was safe, we moved you here.'

'I've been asleep all that time?'

'No. You have woken up every day, and every day I have handed you the newspaper, which you have read, and then, the following morning, you have forgotten. One morning, you will remember. I'm hoping that will be tomorrow.'

'Why do I keep forgetting?'

'You're having trouble adjusting. It will pass.'

'You've tricked me.'

'No. I did as I was asked,' Mercer said. 'Jon said you were amenable.'

'But I'm Jon.'

'No. You are Bill. You have always been Bill.'

'Bill?'

'Yes, Bill.'

'And where is Jon?'

'He is enjoying his new life, with Mark.'

'But Mark is dead.'

'In your life, he is dead,' Mercer said, 'because you killed him. You became exactly what you are. You fulfilled the potential of your nature, gave expression to your rage and hacked him to death. What does that tell you? In Jon's life, the life he wanted, he is back with Mark and they are happy.'

'Mark is not with Matt?'

'Not in Jon's life, he isn't. In Jon's life, after they left the restaurant, Jon went home alone, and Mark and Matt went back to Mark's studio. Before long, though, Mark grew tired of Matt. He finally saw him for what he was—'

'He did?'

'He did,' Mercer said. 'But let us not confuse the issue. In Jon's life, Mark got back with Jon, who takes his pills and sees his doctors just as he should.'

'So, they're happy ever after?'

'No one is happy ever after. They accommodate. They rub along. They do what normal people do.'

'Where are my pills? I need my pills.'

'You won't be needing them anymore,' Mercer said. 'You never paid much mind to them when you should have and now it's too late. Irrelevant, in fact.'

'And what about my life?'

'This is your life now. This is what you wanted.'

'No, it isn't.'

'Yes, it's what Bill chose.'

'I'm Jon.'

'No, you are Bill. You are just having difficulty accepting that.'

'It says in the paper I'm Jon.'

Mercer sighed. 'Don't be obtuse now. Of course to them you are Jon. They don't know anything about our work. But you do. You know that you are not Jon.'

'I want to go back to my flat.'

'Which flat?'

'My flat – that flat.' He stabbed a finger at the newspaper.

'You don't live there anymore,' Mercer said. 'Technically speaking, you never did. Besides, you live here now. You must not think about that flat any longer. It will only cause you distress.'

'I want to see it.'

'You can't see it,' Mercer said. 'It's been boarded up and heavily padlocked. It's a crime scene.'

He, whoever he was, felt a terrible pain in his head.

'I need my pills.'

'I can't agree to that,' Mercer said. 'They won't help now. Not you, not us.'

'I didn't do this.' He pointed at the newspaper.

'All the evidence suggests otherwise.'

'I have to leave here.'

'You can never leave here,' Mercer said. 'You must stay here, always. It is not safe for you to go out. You'll be arrested. They'll send you to prison.'

'I am in prison.'

'You think so?' Mercer looked mildly amused. 'No one's going to bugger you without permission or slash you with razors here. In fact, no one will be intimate with you at all. Ever again.'

'There are people I need to see.'

'Who could you possibly need to see now?' Mercer asked.

Who indeed?

'See, you can't think of anyone. And no one needs to see you,' Mercer said. 'No, it's a fact of life now that no one must ever see you or suspect that you are here, or even that you exist. You must always stay here. No one must smell even a trace that might suggest your existence. That's how unimportant you are. A grub in the food chain.'

'What am I going to live on?'

'All your basic needs will be taken care of – food, clothing and so on.'

'And money?'

'You won't need money,' Mercer said. 'You can't go any-where to spend it. You will earn your keep here.'

He snatched the wallet off the bedside table. It was empty of cash, and the bank card and credit card did not belong to Jon. They belonged to a man called Bill.

'You see,' Mercer said. 'You are Bill and this is your life now. I'll take the cards. You won't need them anymore.'

He handed over the wallet.

'Come with me,' Mercer said, getting up and opening the door leading out of the tiny room.

Mark's studio was little changed, though the kitchen looked much cleaner, and there were new pieces of furniture here and there, most noticeably a long and very old wooden table with matching chairs.

'You bought Mark's studio?'

'I didn't need to,' Mercer said. 'I owned it already. I own the whole building. I have done for a number of years now.'

He remembered the days, good and bad, he'd spent here with Mark. Although, of course, he was now to accept that technically it was not 'here' at all. From now on, that word would have a very different meaning for him, decoupled from a fixed locus in space or time. Here, there, wherever, there'd be no more haphazard afternoon epiphanies. He himself, whoever he was, had seen to that.

Somehow, he had the feeling that Mercer knew what he was thinking. He suspected some compassion, buried deep.

'What happened to Mark's stones?' he dared ask.

'I've had them moved to the basement,' Mercer said. 'They're safe.'

'So, I live here now?'

'You live in there.' Mercer pointed back to the cell. 'Always, only and ever in there. Out here, you serve.'

'Serve who?'

The Chinese screens folded back and Herman got up off the bed.

'Come along,' Mercer said. 'You have work to do.'

He followed into the kitchen.

'I suppose your first task should be to deal with these,' Mercer said, pointing to a plastic tub on the draining board.

'What is it?' he asked.

'Open it and find out.'

He opened it and inside there were two human penises, packed in ice.

Herman, coming up behind them and seeing the contents of the box, clapped his hands, before tapping his knuckles together under his chin, squealing with delight, 'Hot dogs. And eggy soldiers too. With toast.'

'What am I supposed to do with these?' he, Bill, whoever, asked Mercer.

'Put them in the freezer, of course.'

'Can we have jam?' Herman asked.

'With what?' Mercer sounded impatient.

'With everything,' Herman giggled.

Until the knife decides

The ochre piss lay thick and sullen in the bowl. Jack gave himself a hard shake and hit the hangman's bog handle with a practised snap of the wrist, letting loose a shock of water from the rusty cistern that rattled the mottled window pane. Groaning from the pain in his abdomen as he did up his zip, he looked out at Upper Street, where the day was reluctantly opening one eye.

Even now, his eyes missed nothing. He could see dried blood at the spot, at the mouth of the side street, between the off-licence and the Indian restaurant. Other than that, and the flies and wasps assuring themselves it wasn't jam, there were no telltale signs, nothing to record what had happened just a few hours before.

It had been a slick move all right. He'd give him that much. Jacket draped over the right forearm in execution of the good deed, falsely played. And no time wasted crossing the road and turning the corner, well out of sight.

He hadn't been expecting this. Not just yet.

Comes around so quickly.

Jack threw the window open wide and took in a long, deep breath that whistled into his bones, almost cracking a rib.

Not a well man. Not well at all.

Jack didn't know it, but just hidden from his view by the odd, angular relief of the building opposite, Jez was tapping his fingers on the wheel, the engine humming impatiently at the lights, while Helen chewed her lip.

'What if he's there?' Jez asked.

'He may well be there,' Helen said. 'No one said he wouldn't be there. The idea was to get there early—'

'He'll be so hungover, he won't hear us,' Laura said, from the back seat.

Jez looked anxious. 'Does he get drunk every night?'

'Lately he does, yes,' Laura said, thinking surely she'd made that clear by now. 'And a lot more besides.'

'And if he does hear us?'

'Then, I'll have to deal with it,' Laura said.

'Is that a good idea?' Helen asked.

'It's better than anyone else trying to deal with him,' Laura said.

Helen chewed her lip. 'Are you sure you should even be there?'

'Yes. It's better I am, believe me.'

The traffic lights changed and the car slipped into the flow of traffic.

'Do you have much stuff?' Jez asked.

'Not much. It's just a studio flat. It won't take long. Clothes mainly. CDs and things, you know…'

'You have more than that,' Helen said.

'Do I?'

'Yes. Everyone always does.'

'Honestly, I don't.'

'And his place is…?' Jez asked.

'Right underneath,' Helen said. 'Isn't it?'

'Yes,' Laura said.

'Well, we'd better tread carefully then,' Jez said.

'You don't have to do this if you—'

'Yes, yes we do,' Helen said, throwing Jez a warning look. 'And we want to.'

'Thank you,' Laura said.

'It'll be all right,' Helen said. 'It'll be over soon, you'll see. And then you can start over.'

'Yes,' Laura said, not sure just then what that could mean.

Jack washed his hands with the thin tablet of soap and dried them on the threadbare towel hanging on a thick black nail. He walked back down the stairs, sat down and took a moment.

'Did you kill him?' Jack asked.

'I just told you I did.'

Jack reached into the right-hand pocket of his leather

waistcoat, pulled out the leather wallet and opened it. He laid the credit card and bank card on the table.

'Did you kill him?' Jack asked.

'What?'

'Did you kill William R Deal?' Jack tapped the cards.

He said nothing.

'I know he's dead. I checked.'

'I didn't know he'd died. Though, if I'm honest, I didn't fancy his chances. Poor old Bill.'

'His name was William, not Bill,' Jack said. 'William.'

'Poor old William then.'

'Explain how it happened.'

'Another drink.'

'First, you explain.'

'It's your turn.'

Jack leaned over and poured a small measure. He snatched the bone-handled knife from the table, flipped it into the air, caught it by the handle and fired it with great precision at the back door. The blade sliced into the soft wood and hung, gently arcing in the warming morning air, as if considering whether to sound a pleasing note or simply snap in two.

'You've got until it decides,' Jack said.

Factotum

He didn't know how many summers had passed, one or two, maybe three, before he stopped looking in the mirror each morning and telling himself: 'You are not Jon. You have never been Jon.' Not because he had come to accept that he was Bill, although he knew it must be true, but because he found it easier to think that he was no one. Herman never used his name and nor did Mercer when he visited. So he simply became 'he'. He took it as read that he, by return, should never use their names.

He didn't know why his last attempt to measure time should be in summers. He imagined this would surprise everyone who thought they knew him. But he had always loved summer, maybe because he was born at its very height. At least, he assumed he was, because Jon was.

So, one, two or three, he didn't know how many summers,

since they sat down that day at the large wooden table, over coffee, politely enough, for Mercer to spell out to him the rules for living there – rules that applied only to him.

As Mercer spoke, he did his best to pay attention but could not help running his hand, absently, over the ancient varnished surface, grey-brown with deep black wrinkles and gouges, yet smooth everywhere to the touch. Somehow, the sensation gave him comfort, and transported him somewhere else.

As Mercer continued, he saw too – or, more accurately perhaps, understood, from the vantage point of his semi-absence, his half-life – that Herman sat attentive, saying nothing, qualifying nothing, adding nothing. It was immediately clear who had authority here and who submitted.

When Mercer had finished listing the rules, Herman, at his signal, went off to the kitchen to prepare a light lunch, 'something piquant to delight the taste buds'.

'I imagine you might have a question for me,' Mercer said. 'This will be your last opportunity.'

'Can you tell me anything more about Jon?'

'I have told you that he is well.'

'And Mark?'

'Also well. I believe they are what people call "happy".'

'Don't you call it "happy"?'

'When you people say "happy", you are talking, no matter what you may claim and despite all evidence to the contrary, about a permanent condition. But there are no permanent conditions here.'

'No? Just rules, then?'

'Yes,' Mercer said, with a smile that at least seemed free of malice. 'You're catching on.'

'Nevertheless, I'm still glad,' he said, after a moment.

'It's good that you are glad, I suppose. I feared you might grieve forever.'

'I thought you said there were no permanent conditions.'

'There aren't,' Mercer said. 'But sometimes you people never learn.'

'I thought you didn't like to speak in riddles.'

'I rarely speak in anything else.'

'And I didn't see it.'

'You chose not to.'

'You tricked me.'

'You wanted me to trick you.'

'No.'

'Yes,' Mercer said. 'Your type always do. You think you are bigger than the trick. You think you have it all figured out. But when you get behind it and find out what it's really about, then you don't like what you find at all.'

Herman arrived back at the table, bearing plates and bowls.

'What happens to my flat?'

'You mean the crime scene. A young couple will move in shortly,' Mercer said.

'A couple? Is there room?'

'Love makes room, apparently. Now eat.' He waved a hand over the food on the table. 'You will need your strength.'

The rules were simple. He was never to leave the building,

185

and never to be seen by anyone other than Herman and Mercer. No visitors or deliverymen were even to be aware of his existence. For a long time, visitors were non-existent, so that was easy. Deliverymen were frequent and for the most part routine, as that, generally, was how Herman preferred to buy things, because shopping was 'vulgar, dirty, tiresome and for little people with no understanding of the principles of communicable disease'.

When these deliverymen arrived, he was to stay quiet in his room, the door locked, until they had finished their business and gone. He must always lock himself in and slide the key under the door for Herman, who would unlock it when ready. Then, he was to emerge and, without question or prompting, immediately set about sorting whatever they had delivered to its proper place, and tidy as needed.

He was responsible for all cleaning duties, performed according to a strict colour-coded rota on a cork notice board in the kitchen. These included laundry, floor-mopping, toilet scrubbing and sorting rubbish for disposal, and leaving the neatly tied bags by the door at fixed times each week. Only Herman was allowed to take them down to the bins on his way out.

He did not, however, have to cook, because Herman, he soon discovered, fancied himself quite the chef. He even loved baking – 'puff pastries and ripe tarts, specialities of the house'. He, on the other hand, it was somehow understood without ever being said, could scarcely butter bread or open milk, and could even sour water just by looking at it.

At first, surprisingly, he was permitted to eat from the same pot or dish as Herman. It quickly became clear, however, that his nourishment and wellbeing were not Herman's concern. No, his role in this was to ladle on thick, savoury praise from the deepest pan of his self-abasement. That and do all the washing-up. And Herman, it seemed, couldn't boil an egg without using every utensil in every cupboard and every drawer.

Herman used the bone-handled hunting knife for everyday food preparation. And he must make sure to leave it, after washing and drying, at a precise angle, on the breadboard next to the large glass sweet jar full of coins and foreign notes.

'I got this in the army. I loved the army, oh my, yes. That's where I learned to cook,' Herman told him once, licking his lips and wiggling his fat behind in his cook's apron, nicely tied with a bow at the back. 'And the boys loved my cooking, oh yes. I'd send my young scamps off on a day's soldiering with a full-fat fry-up in their young bellies. Nothing gives a soldier a lift on an ice-cold morning like fried eggs, bread and bacon, and one of my big, fat, homemade juicy sausages, with beans and black pudding, toast and butter, mushrooms in season, and a steaming mug of copper-brown tea you could stand pennies on.'

'An army marches on its stomach,' he said, lamely mirroring Herman, because he had learned, early on, that empty, readymade phrases were all that Herman really required of him. He had no interest in what he thought about anything. Words from his mouth served only as a short aural signal for

Herman to recharge and continue his perpetual broadcast of self-love.

'One Christmas,' Herman said, his eyes blinking rapidly, 'I killed a goose.'

'To cook, I assume,' he said, but Herman was so immersed in the memory of it that he did not hear him, or at least he did not detect his tone.

'Long, soft, slender, downy neck, piping blood from a severed artery,' Herman said, rhapsodising. 'Imagine all the things you could do with that.'

He did his best not to.

In return for all of this, in addition to being fed, he was clothed, to the point of functional necessity and no more, and given the shelter of his room and the grace of their protection. He was forbidden to use the computer or the phone – he must not even answer it for Herman.

He was, however, allowed to watch TV in the evenings, though he had no choice over what they watched – Herman, stretched out on the sofa, and he upright on a stiff-backed chair – except when Herman was out, which, at this time, was often.

Herman would laugh hysterically at news of war, murder and catastrophe. The more graphic the images, the louder he squealed, sometimes stuffing a cushion into his mouth to muffle his laughter.

Once, Herman turned to him and said, 'I see that leaving bunches of flowers in public places when people die tragically has become all the rage. We must give it a go, don't you think?

Has there been one lately? A tragedy? Or do we have to make our own? Is that how it works?'

Then, he almost wet himself at the cut of his own wit.

Should he ever hesitate, even fractionally, in his duties, or show the smallest hint of chafing at their tedium, the threat of being handed over to the authorities was summoned with a look, a barely raised eyebrow.

The purpose of all of this, as he understood it, was to ingrain in him the idea that he existed now solely to support Herman in the creation of his great work. So, as he swept and cleaned, wiped and waxed, piling load after load of Herman's soiled underwear and yellowed sheets into the washing machine, the master himself would sit at his desk by the window, drinking coffee and tapping away at the keyboard.

Occasionally, Herman would read a few lines aloud to him, his jowls thick, tongue out, eyes watering, like a dog expecting a bone for fucking the furniture in front of the guests and children.

What persuasive argument could there be for not putting him down? Not one.

Very good, he'd say, leaning on his broom handle, nodding in a monkey's mimicry of admiration that wouldn't have fooled a child. In truth, he had no idea whether Herman's lines were good or bad. Gallons of bleach, detergent and limescale remover had long since rotted his finer faculties. It didn't much matter. It was taken for granted he'd dredge more burned scrapings of unction from the bottom of that deep pan.

Herman would turn and carry on, and so would he, each absorbed in their separate tasks.

In good weather, Herman spent time in the small garden he had created, at the back of the building, sheltered by a high wall from the busy street. He had removed 'tons – *simply tons* – of rubbish and rubble', laying a stone path and planting flowers, shrubs and vegetables. Herman even had a swing erected – just a simple metal frame with an old tyre on a rope – so that, on sunny days, he could sit on it, grinning like a congenital idiot.

He could not see Herman's face so far below, but idiot was his default, his inescapable, expression.

He didn't doubt that this work would have fallen to him, or at least the grunt work, had he been allowed to leave the building. Herman's sour expression told him that this fact was not lost on him, and that there would be payback – more cleaning, more scouring, an unfeasible quantity and variety of utensils dirtied in the simple peeling of a potato.

All this and less, every day less and less, was his fiefdom.

Mercer never defined, however, what Herman could not reasonably expect. The only conclusion, in the circumstances, was that whatever Herman wanted, he'd get. This seemed to be Herman's understanding also. So he lived in dread of the limits of Herman's demands. Thankfully, in the early days, his master showed great restraint. Or maybe, at that time, Herman had no need to hold in check the inner pressure swelling like a noxious gas from a deep, tiny rupture in his inner sewer. Pressure that would later build until it finally ripped him open.

190

No, up to that point, he had only to become familiar with Herman's likes and dislikes, habits and rhythms, routines and tropes, odours and stains, better than he knew his own. When Herman farted, it was he who must cough in apology and open a window.

No matter how odd this arrangement, or limiting or repugnant, he accepted it all the same. He had no choice now but to be guided by Mercer – and, make no mistake, it was Mercer who guided him in all of this; Mercer who had become, for him, authority greater than any other law that society could contrive or enforce; legislature and police of his will.

As for his feelings about Herman, he took the pragmatic view that it was best not to frame them with a name, because that name could only be 'hate'. And look where that had got him.

That, more or less, is how they muddled along without much incident – for how many summers?

Artist in residence

Herman wrote his play in the seemingly unquestioning assumption that Mercer would mount it, as soon as it was ready, at the Panharmonium.

He, meanwhile, assumed that Herman wrote it without intending ever to finish it, because writing it had become the work itself.

So, it was a surprise when, one morning, as he was resting his elbows on his mop, surveying his glistening floors with some pride, Herman marched up to him, as bright as dawn, and said, 'It's done.'

'What is?'

'The play.'

'Congratulations.'

Herman nodded. 'I must tell Mercer.' And off he went, straight to the phone.

By now, he had stopped marking time in normal units, but even the broken mechanism of his inner clock told him that, having been a regular if not frequent visitor in the early days, it had been a while since Mercer had come to call.

Did he care at all about Herman's play? Remember it? He didn't even know the title. Well, so he claimed.

The telephone conversation was brief. Herman had no sooner hung up than he was under his feet again.

'He's coming round,' Herman said.

'When?'

'In three weeks.' The voice trailed away as Herman shuffled off, suspicion and doubt already shadowing him.

It was a long three weeks.

He looked up from mopping the floor to see Mercer standing there, straight as a wall, in one hand a long metal box, like a safety-deposit box, and in the other, gripped tightly, a bunch of drawstring canvas bags.

'Mercer,' Herman said, running from the other end of the studio, the manuscript of his play in his hands.

'You,' Mercer said, ignoring Herman, 'will deal with these.' He hoisted the metal box and set it down hard on the long wooden table, dropping the bags on top in a scattering pile.

'Mercer,' Herman said, 'about the play. I have it here. I wanted to run—'

'The Panharmonium has declared bankruptcy,' Mercer said. 'There won't be any play. There won't be any more plays.'

Herman came to a stop and wobbled like a jelly on a plinth. 'But you promised—'

With his eyes fixed on middle distance, not so much as flickering in Herman's direction, Mercer removed his trouser belt in a single fluid motion and, without saying a word, turned and set about Herman, lashing him face and body, putting his back and shoulders fully into it, until Herman crawled under the table and curled up in a ball, whimpering and bleeding onto the few sheets of his manuscript he had managed to keep hold of, while the rest, crumpled and torn, were scattered and trampled into the floor.

At one point, the belt buckle dug itself into Herman's cheek. Mercer snapped the belt back hard, gouging out a morsel of flesh that flew across the room to hit the far wall and stick there for a moment before plopping onto the shining, disinfected floor. When Mercer had done lashing him, he planted a few full-bodied kicks – one at least to the face, and a couple to the kidneys, hard enough to send shocks deep into the shuddering offal, and ripples upward through the curvature of the spine. Enough, maybe, to cause a deep rupture. Herman coughed phlegm and blood down his shirt, and Mercer came to an abrupt halt, like a man content he'd achieved what he'd set out to, in less time than he might have imagined.

Fastening his belt, once more ignoring Herman, Mercer approached him without losing a beat. 'The creditors have closed in again. The moment has come to move on. Of course, I plan for these contingencies. I keep a healthy portion of my interests liquid.'

'Yes,' he said. 'I remember.'

'Here's what you have to do. It's very simple.'

'OK.'

'These bags are full of money. Mainly notes. Some coins. But it's all money, isn't it?'

'It's all money,' he said, involuntarily looking down at Herman.

'Don't look at him,' Mercer said. 'Look at me. He won't be able to tell you anything useful. You should know that by now.'

'OK.'

'I want you to sort this money. Put all the £50 and £100 notes only – in neat piles, don't mix them – in the metal box, then lock it and keep it on the shelf in your room. Yes?'

'Yes.'

'Separate out the twenties, tens and fives – if there are any fives, there shouldn't be, but tell me if there are – into rolls of twenty, or as many rolls of twenty as the numbers allow, and secure each one tightly with a rubber band. Double-wound is probably best. More secure. Got all that?'

'Yes.'

'Then put the coins in the sweet jar in the kitchen, next to the breadboard. You know the one, where Man-baby keeps his favourite penknife, the one he uses to untie his shoelaces because his fingers are too pudgy – you know the one, yes?'

'Yes.'

'And then...'

'And then?'

'And then,' Mercer said, 'leave the bags, drawn tight at the neck, on the table.'

'On the table.'

'Yes, on the table. I'll collect them when I drop off the next batch, and so on. As I said, simple.'

'Simple, yes.'

'Remember, the metal box stays in your room until it's full.'

'Until it's full.'

'And then?'

'And then?'

'And then,' Mercer said, 'you tell me that it's full. And then?'

'And then?'

'And then, we'll have to see.'

'OK.'

'Excellent,' Mercer said, leaning down to speak to Herman under the table, still whimpering, still bleeding. 'Man-baby?'

'Yes?'

'Man-baby, whatever I promised you, I delivered, didn't I?'

Herman made a strangled whining noise, at which Mercer banged the table hard with the flat of his hand. 'Didn't I?'

'Yes, yes,' Herman blubbered.

'So, I owe you nothing.'

'You owe me nothing.'

'Good, now repeat after me: there will be no play.'

Herman hesitated.

'Repeat.'

'There will be no play,' Herman said.

'No one wants the play.'

Again, Herman hesitated, his hands cradling his bloodied head.

'Repeat.'

'No one wants the play,' Herman said, the words bubbling through blood and snot.

'It's a ghastly little play.'

'It's a ghastly little play,' Herman repeated, the pain of the words choking him.

'It is of no artistic merit or lasting value,' Mercer said, drawing out each word, like a skewer from a wound.

'It is of no artistic merit or value,' Herman repeated, audibly crushed.

'Excellent. Now, the good news,' Mercer said, clapping his hands, 'the very good news is that all is not lost.'

'It isn't?' Herman still did not dare look at Mercer.

'No,' Mercer said. 'I have a plan for you.'

'A plan?'

'Yes, you are to be reinvented.'

'Reinvented?'

'Yes, reinvented – as an artist.'

'An artist?'

'Yes,' Mercer said, grinning viciously, 'isn't that fantastic?'

'But I don't—'

'Oh but you do,' Mercer said. 'You can. You will.'

'I will? I mean, I will.'

'That's the spirit.' Mercer patted Herman's forehead. 'The

even better news is that your first work is ready and waiting to be executed.'

'It is?'

'Yes.' Mercer took Herman by the shoulders, easing him out from under the table and helping him to his feet. He then went to the sink, ran his handkerchief under the cold tap and gave it to Herman to wipe the blood and gunk from his face.

'Where is it waiting?' Herman asked, still too terrified to look Mercer in the eye.

'Downstairs. Now.' Mercer took Herman by the hand. 'Come, come with me and I'll show you. Don't be scared. Everything is going to be fine. You are going to be a very major artist and the world is going to revere you. Mind your step…'

Mercer led Herman out. Would he ever see him alive again?

He took his mop and bucket to the kitchen and then set about sorting the money as Mercer had instructed.

A while later, Herman came back alone, his face a ghost's ghost. For once, he felt sorry for him. Almost.

'Everything all right?' he asked.

Herman said nothing. With a half-shrug and a short gasp, he fell onto a chair at the table.

'I could fill a bowl with warm water,' he said. 'And bathe your face.'

Herman, deep in thought, nodded.

He brought the bowl and, with a fresh white hand towel, patted and dabbed at Herman's face, slowly at first to get the measure of his pain, until he had wiped away all the dried blood, snot and sweat. He then applied antiseptic cream to the cut licked out by the tongue of the buckle and covered it with a plaster.

'There, all better. Yes?'

'Better, yes, much better,' Herman said. 'But I should have a proper bath in a while.'

'In a while,' he said. 'When you've recovered a little.'

He was carrying the bowl and bloodied towel to the kitchen when Herman called out, 'No play, after all.'

'No,' he said, turning. 'No play.'

'But I am to be an artist.'

'Yes, very good. An artist.'

'Mercer has told me what I am to do.'

'Has he?' he asked, careful not to betray any feelings, good or bad, about the matter.

'What I am to create.'

'And what is that exactly?'

'It's an…'

'Yes?'

'…an experimental work.'

'I see.'

'He's even given me a deadline.'

'A deadline?'

'Yes, March,' Herman said. 'The twenty-first.'

'Well, that gives you time, doesn't it?'

'"Now you'll have to pull your finger out," he said.'

'Did he? That was un—'

'"Put your back into it, do some serious work for once in your life."'

'Well, that's—'

'And he's thought it all through,' Herman said. 'He's planned it all. In every detail. He's even—'

He stopped, half-turned. 'Yes…?'

'Never mind.'

'As you wish.' He took a cautious step.

'He's just the fucking agent,' Herman roared at him.

'The agent, yes,' he said, turning fully to face him.

'He sets in motion, but he does not create.'

'No, he doesn't create. You create.'

'I create,' Herman roared.

'Yes.'

'It will be me,' Herman said, 'still me who creates it, who executes it. I am the artist.'

'Of course.'

'I am, aren't I?'

'Yes,' he said, 'you are an artist.'

'I am *the* artist,' Herman screamed.

'You are *the* artist.'

Herman nodded, his eyes searching him, and himself too, for absolute assurance, and finding none. Doubt was spreading through him like a disease.

He smiled weakly at Herman and went into the kitchen.

'I hate him,' Herman cried suddenly, the rage hitting the back of his head like a shovel.

Well, you've learned something at last.

Herman's expression was disfigured by a brute despair he'd never seen in him before, his face almost a negative of itself exposed in flesh. The more he stared at it, the darker it became, an image that somehow clarified his soul in the very process of its own corrosion.

In a second the image, the glimpse, was gone, but he knew all the same that the simple bliss of their domestic routine was at an end.

For whom the bell tinkles

Immediately after Mercer's visit, Herman began to carry himself differently. After a full day's brooding, he became purposeful, calm and focused, busying himself with the initial preparations.

He thought, hoped maybe, that the change would be temporary, but no, he never saw the old Herman again. From that point on, he knew a succession of distillations and dilutions of Herman, each more pungent, more repellent than the last.

For a few days, following many phone calls and trips out, deliverymen came and went with all the speed of the latest thing. This time, however, nothing but stony thuds, bony echoes and hairy-necked grunts made it past the ground floor, where, the frequent double-locking and unlocking told him, all was safely secured. He was left to imagine what might be going on.

It hadn't escaped him that, in all this, Herman had to pass up an opportunity to get his hands dirty on his behalf. Surely, he thought, there'd be payback for that. But where once the spite would have fizzed in Herman's eyes like Champagne in a dirty toilet, Herman now gave every appearance of barely registering his existence. He, however, sensed the ploy: beneath Herman's seeming indifference, cool anticipation lay in waiting – like a fetish, slowly stroked to draw out the finest drops of pleasure latent in the pain imagined, the twists to come.

Not everything was delivered. Sometimes Herman went out, bought things and returned with them by taxi, lugging them unaided into the basement. That alone told him something significant had begun, and still he was not to know about it.

Amid all the furtiveness and heavy lifting, Herman made one other purchase. He was mopping when he heard it for the first time. He turned and there stood Herman, a tiny silver bell held lightly between thumb and finger. Its sudden appearance signalled an unhappy new phase in their relationship. Up to now, it had been mutually understood that he fetch and carry, clean and scrub, spit and polish, with little, if any, need for precise instructions. In the deal struck, a bond of thin civility had tightly glued together their mismatched parts.

'Ask not for whom the bell tinkles,' Herman said. 'It tinkles for thee.'

From then on, everything would be at the bell's command. Each day, and countless times each day, its single note – quick as sharpened steel – would jab the tightened muscles around his eyes, pricking the stinging cornea, finding new nerves to pluck at and tear, threading them into blinding headaches and knotted pains in his hands, legs, arms and back.

Eventually, he had to ask for painkillers. To his surprise, Herman consented. But then, Herman knew, he couldn't really work without them, and that wouldn't do at all. Besides, they didn't kill the pain, simply reduced it to levels that allowed him to carry on working. And, of course, the more he took, the more he needed to take, to ever-lessening effect and Herman's ever-greater pleasure. For Herman, he now knew, adored pain.

So there he was, the analgesic addict, just about to pop a couple more into his mouth when Mercer turned up, only a few weeks after his last memorable visit.

He set more bags of money on the table, nodding in approval at those sitting waiting for him. 'Are you in pain?'

'Yes,' he said.

'That's too bad,' Mercer said. 'Pain is the body's way of telling you that something is wrong.'

'That's very true,' Herman said, approaching in measured steps from the other end of the studio.

'But, of course, not necessarily with the body,' Mercer added, to both and neither of them.

Mercer eyed Herman coolly and, to his surprise, Herman returned the look. Not for long, true, but long enough to seal the crisp, ironic mutual goading that would characterise their relationship from now on.

Mercer seemed, for once, less than completely surefooted. While nobody said anything, and looks remained locked, the suggestion hung in the air that last time Mercer had been lucky – he had caught Herman off guard, but he would never enjoy that advantage again. The next time, there would be consequences, Mercer could be sure of that. Herman may have been as soft as baby squid on a good day, but he was as mad as a butcher in a famine on a bad one. They both knew that.

'We weren't expecting you,' Herman said, breezily, lighting a cigarette.

'I thought you'd given up,' Mercer said.

'So did I.' Herman channelled two blue-grey snakes out of his nostrils, charming them into a dance.

'Well, there was this to attend to,' Mercer said, nodding to the bags on the table, then to him. 'And the box?'

'About one-third full,' he said.

'Excellent.' Mercer seemed content.

'Indeed,' Herman said, his indifference weighed, precise.

'I also wanted to see how things are progressing.'

'Equipment bought and installed, and ready to make a start. Getting the ventilation system in proved tricky. And time consuming.'

'But necessary.'

'Very necessary.'

'And all done now?'

'Got there in the end.'

'Excellent. And you used my list of suppliers? Exclusively?' Mercer said.

'Without the least deviation. Are you staying for lunch?'

'Yes, why not?'

'I'll make a start. Salad with homemade dressing. Mother's recipe.'

Mercer went to speak but Herman was already on his way to the kitchen. It was clear that alternatives weren't on the menu.

'Sit,' Mercer said to him, one hand outstretched, the other pushing the moneybags, still in separate piles, the sorted and the unsorted, to one end of the table to make room.

'I'm not sure,' he said, leaning on his mop. 'I have things to do.'

'Nothing that won't wait, I'm sure.'

He looked towards Herman, who gave a short nod. Mercer paid no attention, his easy manner suggesting that if he was minded to worry about this tiny dent in his absolute authority, he was even more minded not to show it. It could wait.

'Mother's recipe.' Mercer smirked.

He winced.

'Did you know,' Mercer asked, leaning close, dropping his voice to a stage whisper, 'he literally believes his mother was an angel? But she wasn't, you know. She was a sickbed simpleton abused by his drunken, womanising, primate of a father, too paralysed by fear to climb out of her diseased sheets, where she lay for a dozen dull years before she, how shall we put it, finally took flight.'

He showed no interest.

Mercer gestured, as if performing shadow puppetry for an infant. Still he showed no interest.

'Ah, I see,' Mercer said. 'You think you hate me more now than you hate him. I suppose I follow your reasoning. You have to live with him. I don't. You have to pretend to like him – that's to say, you have to pretend not to hate him, or at least you must not show that you hate him. I suffer no such obligation. But you'll see, in time, who you hate the most.'

He said nothing.

'Sad thing is,' Mercer said, 'I actually quite like you and I can't stand him. But, unfortunately, that's the arrangement. It's what you asked for.'

He was about to say it wasn't what he asked for at all, nothing like, when Herman came to the table, bearing bowls, plates and cutlery on a wooden tray. He set them down without ceremony, muttering, mainly to himself, 'Dressing, dressing, dressing, and salad servers, yes, servers, and glasses, yes, glasses too.' He scuttled to the kitchen and back.

'So, what are we talking about?' Herman asked, pouring water from a jug into three glasses.

'Expectations,' Mercer said.

'Whose expectations?' Herman sat down. 'Please, do start.'

'Yours,' Mercer said.

'Mine?' Herman feigned modest surprise and poured the dressing.

'For the work,' Mercer said.

'Oh yes,' Herman said. 'Pepper anyone?'

'Or, to be more precise,' Mercer said, 'for the exhibition of your work.'

'Salt?' Herman asked him, making a deliberate show of disinterest in Mercer. 'Oh yes, where are we exhibiting?'

'Here,' Mercer said.

'Here? Really? Is this place suitable for an exhibition?' Herman asked, and in an aside to him, 'What do you think of the dressing? Too much vinegar or too much mustard? I can't decide.'

'Downstairs will be perfect for the work itself,' Mercer said. 'Spruce the place up when you're through being creative. Move the furniture around up here, install the odd comfy chair for the better-fed critics. Low lighting, candles, suitable background music. It'll be perfect. Oh, and a few extra tables for food and drink.'

'Finger food?' Herman said, wide eyed and open mouthed, allowing another half-egg to fall off his fork, as slobber dripped from the corner of his mouth onto his shirt.

'Well, you could choose to call it that—'

'Shall we have jelly too? Blood jelly,' Herman said. 'A speciality from back home. It's for grown-ups, you know. Real blood.'

'Perhaps not.'

'Eggy soldiers,' Herman squealed, tapping his knuckles together under his chin.

'Definitely not.'

'As you wish, of course,' Herman said. 'But I can do all the food.'

'I thought we'd get some caterers in.'

'Really?'

'Really.'

'Think of the expense.'

'What price the launch of such a major work, for such an important artist?'

'The price of a suitable venue?'

They smiled thinly at each other.

'More dressing, anyone?' Herman broke the deadlock. 'But, where are my manners, I've forgotten the wine. Wine for you, Mercer?'

'A bit early in the day for me.'

Mercer had barely finished speaking before Herman deliberately turned his attention to him. 'Wine for you?'

'Yes, thank you.'

'And, then, of course—' Mercer began to say, but Herman was on his feet and halfway to the fridge.

'Crisp as a nun's habit and just as pure.' Herman popped the cork. 'Perfect for a light salad.' He poured himself, then him, a full glass each.

'There is also the question of getting the right people to attend,' Mercer said.

'The right people? Who are they?'

'Influential people.'

'Of course,' Herman said. 'People of influence. The critics and carpers, the great and the good, the movers and shakers, the greedy and grasping, the parasites and patrons, the luminaries and liggers, those without whom no party is complete, oh yes they must all be there, every kind of cocksucker and cunt, every—'

'My people will handle it,' Mercer said.

'Handle what?'

'Publicity, marketing, invites, all that sort of thing.'

'Oh yes, that's a very particular sort of thing, of which you – and your people – have proven experience. What is it one says these days? A successful track record, yes, that's it. Lovely, hmmm.' Herman took a long slug of wine and sat back in his chair, giving his legs a good stretch. 'I shall leave it all in your very capable hands. Was there anything else?'

'When will you start?' Mercer asked.

'Monday. The perfect day for beginnings.'

'Excellent.' Mercer got up from his chair and grabbed the sorted moneybags. 'Next Monday it is.'

'Leaving so soon?'

'Yes, I have much to do. I shall drop by again soon, with more of this,' Mercer said, waving the bags, 'and to see how things are progressing.'

'Our door is always open,' Herman said, just as Mercer reached it.

'I know.' Mercer stopped and turned to face him. 'I own it.'

Herman grinned.

'I own it, the walls, the floors and all the contents, including the intellectual property, which, of course, includes you and all the mediocrity that can be squeezed – or beaten – out of you.'

Herman coughed and stared at the table.

They waited until Mercer's step had faded away on the stairs.

'Didn't eat his food. No manners that man. I've quite gone off him,' Herman said, tinkling the bell.

He left his wine and immediately started to clear away, avoiding Herman's eye.

They both knew what had just happened. Herman had won the lunch, but lost the war. He could spar all he liked. Doubtless he would again, and he might never let Mercer beat him up again. But Mercer would always defeat him. Herman knew that.

He sensed Herman's mood plunging fast, so he busied himself with cleaning corners already spotless while Herman continued drinking, in silence, at the table.

Later, as evening sifted through the thin tissue of late afternoon, he tried to slip past Herman to get to the kitchen and empty the dustpan.

'My childhood smelt of meat and the heat still lingering on other people's clothes,' Herman said, his voice thick and dark.

He stopped mid-step, turned and looked at Herman, who was rolling his soft hands, one in the other, like grey, overworked dough.

'He ran a market stall,' Herman continued. 'Sold this and that, but butchery and second-hand clothes were his main stock in trade. Cheap cuts, cheap cloth. Local benefactor, some said. Man of the people, some said. Unbeatable prices, all seasons, all weathers. Early morning to late evening, with me in tow, weekends and, oh yes, days "off sick" from school. Unpaid, unwilling, unhappy. Unfit for it, as he never failed to remind me.'

'Who?'

'My father, the great community benefactor.'

'Oh, was he?'

'No, he was a wife-beating, child-fingering hypocrite. Haven't seen him for years. Not since they put him away. Though between you and me, I'd have put him through a mincer and fed him to sewer rats and starving cats. That's what he deserved. He could be dead now for all I know. I do hope so. I do sincerely hope it was painful.'

'I see.'

'The bastard was never done battering me. My head and the wall were well acquainted. Once, I was out for the count for hours. I eventually came round to find he'd terrified my mother – angel that she was – into not taking me to hospital. After I'd been revived, of a sort, he battered me again because my head had left a dent in the wall that he'd now have to fix because I, of course, had "girls' hands for man's work". But he didn't batter my head that time.'

He stared at Herman, as if seeing him for the first time. True, he was broad shouldered and strong, coarse even, but his body was also unwillingly feminine, as if one day he'd noticed voluptuousness advancing uninvited, threatening to engulf him. So he'd thwarted it, enraged by its sheer inappropriateness. It was as if deep, soul-eating shame had triggered a mutation into the wobbling mass of self-hating denial that sat before him, glaring at the near darkness.

'I'm sorry,' he said, anxious for a cue that he might continue on his way to the kitchen.

'Sorry?' Herman looked directly at him. 'Sorry?'

'Yes.'

'Don't think I don't hear your tone,' Herman said. 'I hear it very clearly. You imagine you're so clever. That you're hidden from view. Think again. You are seen and known. And your tone reveals precisely what you are beneath your smug, patronising little pleasantries.'

'And what's that?'

'A know-all, know-nothing nobody. A snide, snippy, slippery little *shit.*' With that, Herman got up, walked around the table, right up to him, and pressed his face to his, breath close.

He flinched.

'I know he favours you.'

'Who?'

'Mercer. Who else? Who else is there, you dumb fuck?'

'I don't think he does.'

'Yes, I see it. I see your eyes whispering to each other behind my back. I have no idea what he sees in you, because I know you for the animal you are. No amount of scrubbing can mask the smell,' Herman said, tilting back on his heels, digging deep into his chest and spitting with extraordinary ferocity straight into his face. The slimy green globule dripped off his cheek like some freakish spawn.

Right there and then, he would happily have stood on Herman's bloated, self-satisfied face, applying just enough pressure to split the skin, until the fat oozed out. He'd scoop it up, stuff it down his throat and watch him choke on it.

He hated Herman. More than anyone or anything. Mercer had been right.

'Get on with your work,' Herman said.

'Yes, I was just—'

'I speak, you don't.' Herman raised his fist and smashed him to the ground.

He picked himself up and gathered his dustpan and brush.

'Clean up that mess,' Herman said, turning to lift the bottle and the glass from the table, retreating to his bed behind the Chinese screens.

One day, he thought, as he wiped the table clean with a bleached cloth, one day, when you're sitting in your chair, idling in the contentment of your corruption, I'm going to slip up behind you, reach around, plunge my fingers deep into your bucket of blubber and rip out your larynx.

We'll see who speaks then. I never forget. I never forgive. You'll see.

Bad Samaritan

The knife clattered to the ground, the blade unbroken. Jack fixed him with a look.

'So, he's Bill now, is that right?' he asked.

'That's right,' Jack said. 'And you're not.'

'Aren't I?'

'You know you're not.'

'Do I?'

'You do.'

'How's that then?'

'As I told you, while you were sleeping, I phoned a friendly woman. A very friendly woman at Mr William R Deal's bank, to let them know I had his wallet. There was a pause and the very friendly woman put me on hold.'

'Did she now?'

'She did, for quite a while,' Jack said. 'Finally, she came

back on the line. She asked for my name and number, so I gave them. I had no reason not to. I asked if she would be phoning me back. She said someone would call.'

'And did someone call?'

'Someone did,' Jack said. 'Can't remember what his rank was now. High up, anyway. In the police, that is. Did I mention it was the police?'

'You didn't, as it happens.'

'Forgive my lack of attention to detail. It's been a long night,' Jack said. 'Anyway, this high-ranking police officer called me back. Who was I, he wanted to know, and how did I come to be in possession of Mr Deal's wallet? Well, of course, I explained who I was and what I did and—'

'And?'

'And that I had found Mr William R Deal's wallet lying in the street outside my shop. "And where is your shop, Mr Cronin?" he asked. So, I told him. Not far, it turns out, from the narrow side street off Upper Street, between an off-licence and an Indian restaurant, where William R Deal, a visiting American hoping for residency, was stabbed by a mugger as he stood chatting with his lady friend, simply trying to decide where they should go for something to eat on a sunny Saturday evening. With his lady friend who told the police that the assailant was a white man, she thought, who ran off in the direction of Islington Green, the Essex Road, maybe, she couldn't be sure. Well, how could she be sure, given what had just happened? His lady friend, who said it was all over before she even knew it was happening. His lady friend, who said they had only recently met at a drama school. His lady friend, who held his hand as she, and several passers-by who had stopped to help, waited for the ambulance to arrive. Which, of course, it did, but, unfortunately, not in time for William R Deal, who died from his wounds not long before I made my call. So, naturally, the police alerted the bank to flag up any activity on his cards. And then up I pop, Jack-in-the-Box, cards in hand. Imagine their interest.'

'So how come they haven't been here?'

'Because, as a well-respected local trader and businessman, my details check out,' Jack said. 'And because they're expecting me to drop by later today, to hand in his wallet and cards and provide a sworn, signed statement consistent with the details I gave over the phone. Of course, I could get them round here a lot sooner. Now, if you like. That's very much up to you.'

'I didn't kill him.'

'No?'

'No. In fact, I was one of the passers-by you mentioned – who stopped to help.'

'So you're a Good Samaritan in all of this?'

'That was my intention.'

'Intention?'

'To help – but it didn't quite work out as planned. I kind of helped myself.'

'To what?'

'To his wallet.'

'So, bad Samaritan. Tut-tut,' Jack said.

He looked at the knife, weighing the odds.

'Careful now,' Jack said. 'You can barely stand and you're heavily under the influence. Think long and hard about what you want to do. Before you do it.'

'You're well lashed yourself, old man.'

'I've been at this a lot longer than you,' Jack said. 'If it's a sprint over to the door you're wanting, I'm happy to oblige.'

He weighed that up also. True enough, Jack looked lithe, light on his feet, quick and darting.

'I didn't plan it,' he insisted. 'It was just something that happened.'

'How?' Jack asked, rapping the table with his knuckles. 'Tell me how this thing just happened to you on your way here yesterday.'

'I'd rather not rake it all up. Not a happy memory, if you must know.'

'Try your hardest. It's in a good cause.'

'What cause?

'A moment of unvarnished truth.'

'Unvarnished? It'll rot in the rain.'

'It isn't raining.'

'I'm praying it fucking will.'

'Then let us join in prayer. I'm used to the smell of rot. You might even say I like it.'

He stared at Jack, mouth open. No comeback to that one.

'The truth.' Jack rapped the table again. 'Now.'

'Truth is, I woke up with the worst hangover I've ever had. No, truth is, I wasn't hungover, because I was still off my face.

Truth is, I can't remember when I last wasn't. Truth is, there was only one thing on my mind.'

'And what was that?'

'Pack and go.'

'Why?'

'Because it was over.'

'What was?'

'Me and Laura.'

'Why?'

'Because I knew it was an abortion, not a miscarriage.'

'How did you know?'

'Because the bear told me.'

And the thief lay down with the bear

Things had gone very quiet in her flat, so he went up to check on her. He was worried that, after what had happened, there might have been complications or something. He knocked on her door and when she didn't reply, he forced it and let himself in. She was gone. He could see immediately that she'd only packed her small bag, because she was very tidy. Everything had its place, and her small bag, which lived on top of the wardrobe – well, it was gone.

But she'd left the rest. So he thought to himself, why would she leave without telling me? He immediately started to get suspicious. He'd already had the first few drinks of the day, and smoked some big ones, so that just made him even more suspicious.

Then he saw she'd left the teddy.

Why would she leave that, the very thing he bought

specially for her, to make her feel better after she lost the baby?

He took the teddy downstairs and sat him on the pillow, poured himself another, rolled a fat one, lay back on his bed and looked Teddy straight in the eyes.

'I can see you're feeling awkward, trying not to look at me, Ted. I can see you're feeling guilty or something. Don't lie to me now. You tell your old mate the truth.'

And that's when Ted told him that she didn't have a miscarriage. That she'd had an abortion.

'Why though? Why did she do that?'

'Because she didn't want your Devil's drops inside her,' Ted said. 'She didn't want any more of you to seep into the world and poison the house of flesh.'

'But that was my baby. My proper place in the world, Ted.'

'I know. But you begat a bastard. To propagate ruin. You know that's the truth.'

'Where's she gone then?'

'You know where she's gone.'

'Fucking Helen and Jez?'

'Yes.'

'Fucking Helen and Jez. Interfering cunts.'

'Too right,' Ted said. 'You should go round there. Start a ruck.'

'Mate, I don't know where they live. She was clever. Always kept that from me.'

'Phone them.'

'I don't have their number. She kept that from me and all.'

'Sounds like she kept a lot from you.'

'She did, Ted, now that I think about it.'

'Sounds like she didn't love you at all.'

'You know what, my furry friend, I think you might be right about that. What do you think I should do?'

'Pour yourself a large one,' Ted said, 'and roll another fat one, and then, when you're properly in the mood, call her on her mobile and let her know how much you fucking hate her, and how you wouldn't even rent her womb to have a baby. Tell her you'll find some other whore to do the job.'

'I think I'll do that. You're a pal, aren't you? Me old mucker. I can always count on you.'

'Anytime.'

'You can go back to sleep now.'

'Thanks, I think I will.'

'Ted?'

'Yes, mate?'

'You're a snitching two-faced cunt.'

Then he ripped Ted's head off and hurled it at the wall.

He woke up feeling like he had an axe in his head. He looked around his room. It was torn apart.

Time to pack and go. Time to move on.

He remembered calling her when he was totally off his face. He couldn't remember what he'd said.

He checked her flat again to see if she'd come back. She hadn't.

He headed back downstairs and out to the shed in the garden. When he'd moved in, he'd asked the landlord if it was OK to keep his suitcase in there. The landlord said 'no problem'. When he was putting the suitcase on the shelf, he noticed an old tea chest and thought to himself, that'll come in handy one day.

That day had come.

Now there was a lot more stuff piled in there – an old fridge, rusty cooker, a dirty mattress, oil cans, petrol, rusty gas cylinders, tools and tiles, that kind of thing.

A right load of old tat, all of it.

His suitcase was up on the highest shelf, wedged in tight. No easy way to get at it. Well, he wasn't feeling too clever, and had never been that patient, so he just threw himself in there and made a grab at it.

He heard a loud rip, looked up and saw a great big tear in the side of the case.

Fuck, fuck, fuck and cunting fuck.

Next thing, there was an almighty racket. The whole shelf came crashing down – hammers, nails, spanners, drills, the whole lot, and a dirty great spade that'd been hanging on a hook.

He felt a sharp pain in the back of his head. Looked around, saw the spade lying at his heels. Reached up, felt the back of his head. Just glanced him. Could have been a lot worse.

He went to pick it up and finish demolishing anything left standing when his legs went right from under him. He just about fell out the door as the whole lot came crashing down. He crawled out onto the grass and dragged himself over to the bumpy bit between the swing and the tree. He lay on his back. Everything turned white, yellow and silver.

To his left, he saw a man walking down the hill towards the fence, nice and slow, slow as you like. The man stopped at the fence.

Then he thought to himself, this makes no sense. There is no hill. Just next-door's garden on one side and the street on the other.

'Been here before, haven't you?' the man said.

He tried to look up. Tried to speak. But everything was dark and light, light and dark. His lips moved but nothing came out.

'Never learned before. Haven't learned this time,' the man said, disappointed. Then he turned around and walked back up the hill.

Next thing he remembered, something green – maybe a frog, maybe not – hopped onto his face and woke him. He was still on his back, on the same bumpy bit of dirt. It was later. A lot later. He couldn't tell how much later exactly, but he just knew he'd been there for hours because he sort of remembered feeling cold, then very hot, then cold again.

He pulled himself to his feet, still wobbly. The shed door was hanging open. It was a landslide in there. Suitcase ripped, tea chest smashed in down one side. A right mess it was, the whole bloody lot.

Well, that's that plan fucked.

His head was going round and round, and he felt sick, but instinct told him, pack and go. Before Laura or anyone else gets back.

Didn't want to see her now. Didn't want her to see him.

He went into his flat, grabbed a few things off the dresser – keys, money, not much, loose change mainly, looked at the wallet on the side and thought, no, that one's past its best-by date. He checked in the mirror to see if he looked as bad as he felt, and decided he did but not quite as bad as he deserved. He'd just about pull it off, if he took it nice and slow.

And then something—

He couldn't remember.

He headed straight for the Angel, with one thought on his mind. Have to pack it all away.

He wandered down Upper Street in a bit of a panic, a bit of a blur, thinking to himself where could he get what he needed. And what did he need exactly and what was he going to get it with, because he only had a few quid left.

And then—

What the fuck's going on?

He looks down and right in front of him he sees people on their knees. A woman's crying. She's near hysterical. She's holding a man's hand. A man on his back, unconscious, very pale – and his shirt, the bottom half of it, is covered in blood. There's tissue paper, loads of it, soaked in blood, and he can't help thinking of the day his mother threw up all over the table after she'd eaten beetroot. He feels sick again.

Next thing, without thinking about it, he's knelt down beside the woman. He sees the leather strap hanging loose off the man's shoulder. He looks at her.

'He cut his bag with a knife,' she says. 'He tried to fight him off. He cut his bag with a knife. He tried to fight him off. He cut his bag with a knife.'

She keeps repeating it, as if that's what matters, but he knows what's going through her mind. He feels for her, just then. He really does.

Someone says, 'An ambulance is on its way.'

Sure enough, before long, it turns up. And when it does and everyone is distracted, the opportunity presents itself, so he seizes his moment, draping his jacket over his right forearm, snatching the wallet he's seen half-hanging out of the man's back pocket, into the cup of his hand and straight into his pocket.

As they lift the man onto the stretcher, he brushes against him and blood smears his shirt on the left-hand side. He steps back.

No one's noticed. No one's paying him any attention. Why would they?

The man is barely into the ambulance before he's halfway across the street, dodging through the traffic. In a heartbeat, he's turned down Camden Passage.

Next thing, he's looking through a window at a great big trunk.

That'll do. I'll get it all in there.

Jack gathered up the cards, put them in the wallet and put it back in the right-hand pocket of his leather waistcoat.

'Thing is,' he said. 'Don't know what I was thinking really.

That trunk's no fucking use to me at all. Not thinking straight, I suppose. No great surprise, all things considered.'

'So that's it?' Jack asked.

'That's what?'

'That's how it happened.'

'Oh, yeah, that's it,' he said. 'That's how this thing happened to me on the way over here yesterday.'

'No detail you've overlooked?'

'None that I can think of.'

'So, you didn't kill our American friend?

'He wasn't my friend.'

'Clearly.'

'I didn't kill the man.'

'But you didn't hesitate to take advantage. To take what didn't belong to you, from a dying man.'

'It was too good an opportunity to miss. My instincts kicked in.'

'Instincts?'

'An inner voice.'

'And what,' Jack asked, 'did that inner voice tell you?'

'Never turn down a gift.'

'A gift?'

'That's right. Never look a gift horse in the whatever.'

'A gift? Who from?'

'Who the fuck knows? Anyway, seems to me I'm not the only one round here who takes what doesn't belong to him.'

'Is that so?'

'The tat in there belonged to other people. Said so yourself.'

'All obtained fairly and squarely. Legally.'

'House clearances, skips, the bereaved and all that, yeah, you said. Does that include the Chinese screens? Or that knife? Or the sweet jar full of coins by the door? Or the—'

'Ah, those,' Jack said.

'Yeah, those. I'm curious how you came by them.'

'Ah now, those,' Jack said. 'The fox led me to those.'

'The fox?'

'He wanted me to redeem them.'

'Did he now?'

'He did.'

'And why's that then?'

Jack smiled, filled both glasses, emptying the bottle, and pushed one glass towards him.

For the first time, he felt afraid to have another.

'Quid pro quo,' Jack said. 'Quid pro quo.'

He looked down to his left, at the stain on the ground, sticky now, slowly drying. He raised the glass to his lips and took a sip.

Work in progress

'There's a turd on the toilet floor needs seeing to,' Herman said, straightening his tie, admiring himself in the mirror. 'Actually, there's a turd in here needs seeing to. Don't know why I haven't hosed it away long ago.'

'A turd?' he asked, clutching his sides and banging his head on the floor, to distract himself from the pain.

'Yes, one of mine,' Herman said. 'I was experimenting with new ways of sitting while shitting. It didn't quite work out. But it was amusing all the same, and that's all that matters. And there'll be more, because I'm not done. Experimenting, that is, not shitting. For the moment, anyway. Obviously. And the bathroom needs cleaning, again.'

He writhed on the floor.

'What are you doing down there?'

'It's my liver. I think it's failing. Diseased.'

'Nonsense,' Herman said, kicking him hard in the ribs. 'How could that possibly be? You don't drink or take drugs. I don't let you.'

'I've taken too many painkillers.'

'No one forces you to.'

'I need to.'

'Why?'

'Because I am always in pain.'

'Rubbish,' Herman said. 'You take them because you like taking pills. Because you can't take the ones you used to take anymore, the ones you were supposed to take but didn't bother. And look where that got you.'

'Why can't I have them now? I need them.'

'Because that was part of the deal you made.'

'I don't remember that.'

'Well now, you're not really best placed to testify as to what you do and do not remember, are you?' Herman kicked him again. 'Are you?'

'No.'

'That's better. Some sense out of you at last. Some mornings, I don't know, you really are quite the imbecile. What are you?'

'An imbecile.'

'*The* imbecile.' Another kick.

'*The* imbecile.'

'Better,' Herman said, dabbing at his eyebrows with the spittle on his fingers. 'Oh, and there's a small lake of piss too. No particular reason. Just couldn't be bothered. I get the distinct feeling you've been slacking lately. Not enough to occupy you, apparently. Seems now, in addition to the many other burdens you place on me, you expect me to create work for you. Like I was the government or something.'

'I'm always busy.'

'You're a feckless, lazy little shit. You eat me out of house and larder. And just how much toilet paper do you get through, you incontinent little slapper? Has your colon collapsed or something? Doesn't come cheap, you know. Not even recycled.' He smoothed his lapels, picking off tiny threads. 'Make sure it's all cleaned up by the time I get back.'

'Usual time?'

'I imagine so. I'm off to see some friends. Lovely place, close to the park.'

'It'll be done.'

'And the rest, too, and be certain that it is. And don't even think about not doing it for any reason at all, least of all any of your imagined illnesses. Or I might have to start pissing on you. Or in you. After all, what's a bucket for? Eh?'

'Yes.'

'Yes what, you cretin?'

'For pissing in.'

'Just so,' Herman said. 'So, everything ship-shape when I get back, yes?'

'Yes.'

'Very good. Or do we have to break another finger? Or was it a thumb?'

'Finger.'

'Really?'

'Yes.'

'Show me.'

He wiggled the disjointed finger as best he could behind his back.

'Don't forget that you have other bones I could get to work on.'

Another kick, hard this time, and Herman made to leave.

'I can't do anything like this,' he said.

Herman stopped. 'Why not?'

'The rope.'

'Oh, I suppose.' Herman bent down to untie the rope around his wrists.

'Thank you.'

'Ship-shape.' A tinkle of the bell and Herman was gone.

He hung the rope back on its hook on the wall by the kitchen. It was a recent innovation. When Herman was in the mood, he would be told to fetch it so that his master could experiment with tying him up in a variety of positions designed to put maximum stress on the muscles, bones and joints, ankles to wrists behind the back, that sort of thing, and leave him for hours at a time, maybe longer. He'd read about it in a book, Herman told him one day, with that look in his eye.

Everything Herman did now was an experiment of some kind, 'in the spirit of his work'. And it was only during episodes of abuse that they exchanged words at all these days.

He stayed out of Herman's way unless given no choice, when the fountain of malice overflowed and drenched him.

They lived according to a new pattern, no longer eating together or even the same food. He must – if he 'really must' – see to himself with 'whatever's left', but only when it did not inconvenience or offend.

'The way you eat is uniquely but uninterestingly revolting,' Herman told him. 'An insult to the microbial life forms that deserve to consume humanity far more than humanity deserves to consume the planet. I should steep you in bleach and leave you by the door overnight.'

They no longer watched TV together, and even when Herman was out, he would not watch it alone, nor dare to dent the cushions and leave a lingering heat signature to ignite Herman's fury. He no longer wanted to watch TV anyway. Its relentless imagery had become for him a pantomime that made his head hurt, its very presence was a coarse presumption of intimacy he found nauseating. Nor could he endure any longer Herman cackling at calamity, and there was no shortage of that.

He would have liked to read, but he'd read all the books and no new ones were ever likely to appear. Besides, reading was slacking that earned a thump to the back of the head.

In the main, he went about his duties with unquestioning automation, with all thought as to what they aided stowed below, the trap pressed shut, the strain greater every day. Duties that included making preparation for an evening with another guest.

He took a bottle of Herman's preferred, inexpensive, white wine and put it in the fridge to chill, alongside the food he had prepared. He then took a bottle of the preferred red, equally inexpensive, opened it and left it on the side to breathe. He wiped down the wooden table, left out two plates, two white-wine glasses and two red, cutlery, coffee cups and saucers, salt, pepper and condiments. He plumped the cushions, shook the dust out of throws and covers, dusted and polished, and restored order to the CD rack, leaving one or two of Herman's favourites ready to hand.

He attended to the turd and the lake of piss, leaving bathroom and toilet gleaming and fresh, with clean towels on the heated rails. He mopped the studio from one end to the other and back again.

As he was finishing, he slowed to a kind of shuffling dance, cradling the shaft of the mop and interleaving his feet into its straggly grey head, guiding himself into one corner, where he stood a while, eyes closed, humming to himself, lightly rocking, tapping his head on the wall. He did this often now, when Herman was out. It brought him peace and relieved the pain. He could have stayed there until he died. But Herman finding him like that would be a serious mistake, so, somehow, his inner clock, what was left of its diffuse mechanisms, told him when enough was enough.

He went to his room. He sorted Mercer's latest batch of moneybags, and when he'd done, the metal box was almost full. Then, he lay on the bed for a while, with the door to his room open, to get as much air as he could in the time permitted. Knowing Herman would soon return, he locked the door, placed the key on a piece of thin card and slipped it under the door.

Sometimes, he slept through it. Sometimes, the sound of Herman arriving home with company woke him. Other times, it would be the music, chat and laughter. Sometimes, he would not sleep at all. And sometimes, it was the silence following the struggle. By now, however, Herman was well practised. Any struggle was brief, like a bullet too swollen in the barrel to discharge.

This particular night, it was the sound of dragging, followed by the thuds fading on the stone steps and the unlocking below. He heard the door close again, the double locking and the rising steps. Herman then had a shower. Minutes later, he heard his wet feet padding to the door to slip the key back under. He waited until he heard Herman open out the Chinese screens to shield his bed. He waited another minute to be sure he was in it and probably already asleep. Only then did he get up.

He unlocked the door and in the low lamplight took the dishes to the kitchen and loaded them into the dishwasher. He put the empty bottle in the recycling bin and the white back in the fridge, emptied and washed the ashtrays, plumped the cushions, shook out the throws, restored order to the CD rack, wiped down the table and quietly swept around it. He sorted the clothes dumped on the floor by the laundry basket into two piles: Herman's, which he knew by sight and smell; and, of course, the other – the guest's.

In the morning, he was up before Herman, as always. He laid the table for breakfast and washed and dried the clothes from the night before. He ironed Herman's and left them neatly folded on a stool in the kitchen. He folded the others and left them in the waxcloth bag. He was mopping the bathroom floor when he heard movement behind the screens. He cleaned the shower and was out of there in time for Herman to wash, shave and get ready for the day.

'Off to market,' Herman called, a while later, the waxcloth bag over his shoulder. It required no response. He returned after an hour or so, took a handful of coins from his pocket, muttering something about what 'a tight-arse that Grant, that grubby, low-rent, market-stall whore' had become, dropped them into the old sweet jar and hung the empty waxcloth bag on its hook. Herman then changed into his 'artist's clothes' and went downstairs.

He went to the window and looked down onto the small garden, the dead plants and the abandoned swing. A few moments later, Herman emerged with the wheelbarrow, cutting a zigzagging path. Even from that height, he could see him strain as he tipped it up, emptying the sludge onto the barren topsoil. He took the rake resting against the wall and dragged its dirty teeth back and forth until the sludge had been evenly mixed with the dry soil and the trash blown in on the wind. Setting the rake back against the wall, he walked over the fresh patch, smoothing and turning it with his boots until satisfied he had restored an even greyness, with no signs of disturbance or hope of growth. He took the wheelbarrow back inside.

As usual, Herman stayed below for several hours, labouring away, while he was left to get on.

This, of course, wasn't last night's. This was the previous one. Maybe even the one before him. It took time to reduce them to this. He'd lost count of how many there'd been, and after this one, he pretty much lost track of everything.

Herman was out, or down below, he wasn't sure which. He had some recollection of him saying that he needed just two more pieces to complete the work. Even for Herman, he sounded odd, odder than usual. It might have been that morning or some time before. He could not remember.

He'd been shuffling, with the mop, towards his favourite corner for his usual comfort when he saw the contrail of an aeroplane in the clear, blue sky. He stopped, let the mop fall to the floor and went over and fell onto the sofa.

The room shrank from him. He followed the contrail against the deep blue. Written in its vapour, for the world to see, was the terrible thing they had become.

'But why can't you stop it, young man?'

'I can't stop it because I didn't start it,' he said.

'Who did?'

'Jon started it,' he said. 'I'm not Jon. I'm Bill.'

'And can't Bill finish it?'

'No, he doesn't have the strength.'

'I see.'

'And why did he start it, do you think?'

'Because he was tired of being judged. It broke him.'

'Judged?'

'Yes.'

'Who judged him?'

'Everyone.'

'What for?'

'For being unmade, unbecome. Anger destroyed him. He did not become. He devolved.'

'I see.'

'It was all planned, you know.'

'And who planned it?'

'I can't say.'

'Why not?'

'The evidence is there, but it is hidden. Most of it is wrapped in secrets, but some of it is not. A lot of it is written. But some of it is not. In that way, it stays hidden in the ladders.'

'The ladders?'

'The ladders of creation, creation's language. They wrap around each other and write everything on the reality parchments. They are infinitely small and stored in a box, also infinitely small, full of emergent universes. Don't tell everyone. They will be terrified. Because it is true and it is not true.'

'I think I need to see you, young man,' the voice said, the bedside burr warming.

'I can't ever see you, Dr Fisher.'

'Why not?'

'I can't ever leave.'

'Why not?'

'It's locked.'

'The door?'

'Yes, the door.'

'Have you checked?'

'Yes,' he said.

He sensed Dr Fisher did not believe him.

'How did you get this number? How did you know I was here?' he asked.

'You called me, Jon,' Dr Fisher said. 'Don't you remember?'

He saw the open wallet lying on the table, with Dr Fisher's card next to it. 'I'm not Jon. I'm Bill.'

'But if you're Bill, how do you have my number?'

He thought for a moment. 'Jon and I lived the same life.'

'I see.'

'Not the same exactly,' he said. 'Very similar.'

'So…?'

'So, he probably met Dr Fisher too.'

'I see.'

He fell silent.

'Hello, are you still there, young man?'

'Yes, but you sound very far away. There's static and other voices.'

'Ignore the other voices. I'm probably not so very far away. I could be there in under an hour, maybe. Would you like that?'

'Are you on the plane?'

'What plane?'

'Can't you hear it?'

'No, where is it?'

'It's up there,' he said. 'And I'm on it. I have always been on it. I have to go, Dr Fisher.'

'Where are you going?'

'I have to go.'

'Why do you have to?'

'It's ringing.'

'What's ringing?'

'The bell is ringing.'

'What bell?'

'It's ringing, Dr Fisher,' he said. 'I have to go now. It's been nice talking to you.'

'It's been nice talking to you too, young man,' Dr Fisher said. 'Maybe you'll call me again later.'

'Maybe I will, Dr Fisher.'

'And we can have a proper talk.'

'Yes, a proper talk. That would be nice.'

He hung up. It was ringing very loudly now, the bell, but Herman hadn't come back. Or else he couldn't see him.

He fell to the ground. The side of his head came loose, like a broken fire escape, the rivets ripping out of a collapsing wall, scattering the contents of his head like burning rubble all over the floor, torching the room and drawing the pungency of dissolution out of every morsel of wood, stone and metal.

The continuous ringing woke him. It was late evening, maybe. Herman stood over him in silhouette, phone in hand.

'If you're wondering why I haven't beaten you for this,' Herman said, his voice oddly metallic, 'until you bleed out, it's because I no longer have the energy or the patience to loathe you. Or even the need.'

He could not make out anything clearly. The bell continued ringing, reaching an unbearable pitch, constantly shattering and remaking itself into a more intense frequency, screeching like a saw on bone, grinding through to the marrow. A discharge of metallic feedback crackled between his skull and the fat of his brain. He smelt his cortex cindering, ignited by the friction of thought. The fan belt had burnt. The ventilator shuddered to a halt. His mind was melting, dripping out of his nose, cordite corroding the septum, scalding the nostrils and burning his lips. They peeled off, fell to the floor and opened and shut in silent pleading, blue then white.

He crawled into the kitchen, hands over the sides of his head, squeezing the pressure out of the middle ear, where it felt like a nail had been shot deep into the drum. He fell on his side, tongue hanging out the side of his mouth like an eel ripped out of water, blood's metal trickling down his throat.

The distortion stopped and a voice called to him, a small, sweet voice, repeating his name over and over. He came to a dead stop by the laundry basket. He looked down at a fresh pile of clothes, the heat still lingering. He saw a bra, a sleeve-less top and a pair of stockings. He picked up the tiny T-shirt with a drawing of an onion on it, and emblazoned across it: 'I've got layers, peel me.'

Tommy called to him from below. For the first time since he'd woken that morning in his cell, the day Mercer set out the rules, he walked downstairs, following Tommy's cries to the basement door. The padlock hung loose on its rusted, hooked finger. Inside, he saw Herman close the lid of the trunk, turn quickly and sit on it, facing him, arms folded, a black smile.

Tommy's voice stopped.

'Let him out,' he said.

The ventilator chugged away on the wall but the toxic fumes and the stench were almost suffocating, their emissions written in brown waxy layers on the whitewashed walls and ceiling. All around lay bits of wood, wire and metal, large glass bottles, rags and tools. A rubber apron and a gas mask were draped over a plain wooden chair covered in marks, stains and scratches. On a three-legged stool, a claw hammer took its rest.

In the far corner, he saw huge metal drums, buckets, rubber boots and gloves, a stirrup pump, and an intricate mess of metal and rubber tubing. A steel bath was full to the brim with a thick, blackish-red substance. Here and there, odd morsels resisted corrosion, bobbing on the surface, like gristle in a stew. On one thin flap of flesh, he could just make out a crude tattoo of a dove with the word 'Eddie' underneath.

'Let him out,' he said again.

'Let who out?'

'The child.'

'What child?'

'The boy. Tommy.'

'There's no boy here.'

'He's in the trunk.'

'Is he?'

'He was calling for me.'

'He's not calling now.'

'Let him out.'

'He's wrapped in a blanket,' Herman said. 'Quietly sleeping. For ever.'

'He's not sleeping. I hear him crying.'

'Would you like to see him?' Herman slid off the trunk and stepped away. 'All yours. You can take him out if you want to.'

He shook his head.

'There's no lock,' Herman said.

He couldn't open it, couldn't look. He left the basement and went to the main door. He opened it and looked back, expecting Herman to come after him, but he didn't. For the first time in two or three summers, maybe more, he stepped outside, and ran.

The ragged fox of Highgate

He ran, springing lightly on the soles of his feet, as if bouncing on the band of summer itself, taut from end to glorious end.

Was it summer again? He had no idea. But he knew where he was going. The memory was in the body. It couldn't have been in the mind. That hadn't functioned properly for some time. So it must have been the body that held on to things long after the mind had surrendered its grip. It must have been the body, not the mind, that took him from Old Street, up New North Road, or maybe the other way, up City Road; yes, probably that way, the homing instinct kicking in, and then, one way or the other, on to Highbury Corner and the full stretch of Holloway Road and Archway, all the way up to Highgate Wood.

It was late, but he found his way deep into the wood, scrambling through soil and leaves towards an opening in the ground. Surely it was waiting for him. Surely, it was meant for him. He reached it. He looked down. It sucked him in.

He fell down a deep shaft of molten clay, a tower of compacted, disfigured faces, one, at least one, to every grain of earth. They spoke to him. Some begged for release. Others whispered that he had joined them now and would never leave. Others screamed.

He hit the bottom and the darkness doubled in density, like impossibly black water filling his eyes, nose and mouth, pressing him through the hot topsoil, and down deep into it, diffusing him throughout it, until he had no memory, no sense of name, self or life lived. Until he had become microbial, lower maybe, the lowest level of consciousness, aware only of an eternity of thick, dark, immovable mud.

After an eternity without sleep had passed, a pinprick of light appeared in the mud. He moved towards it, eventually emerging out of total darkness into lesser darkness. At this stage, he was in no sense yet really 'he'.

Another eternity passed and a shape asserted itself out of this lesser darkness: the roof of a chamber of earth.

Eternity passed again and he sensed a shadow on the ground, extending from a body that he, finally, somehow, had come to understand as his own. By now, he was in some small measure recognisably 'he'.

He then spent an eternity paralysed in the shadow he came to understand as his own, in as much as he owned nothing, and knew that.

Sight slowly evolved and adjusted to the lesser darkness. From behind a rock, something moved towards him, an enormous animal on all fours. It reached him, stopped and sat on its hindquarters and looked down at him. Unable to move, he looked up to see it looking down, mouth snapped open, saliva dripping from its teeth and jaws onto his face, into his eyes, cleansing them, and into his mouth, purging his gut, squeezing out the digestive juices, greenish, yellow and black.

The animal blinked, its green eyes worlds rotating in their sockets, in a universe of fur, each blink a millennium.

He closed his eyes.

When he woke up, he saw he was lying in a fox's den. The fox leapt down from the earth above, stepped over him and scratched at the dirt. It uncovered in the floor of the cavern a deep cache of eggs, hundreds, maybe thousands, of eggs.

The fox scooped some of the eggs into its mouth and dropped them on the ground next to him, without breaking a single one.

These are for you, its eyes seemed to say. Eat up. Waste nothing.

It stepped over him again and hopped up out of the den.

He ate every last one. Cracked them in his hands and swallowed them in a gulp. Then he ate the shells.

The fox brought more, and he ate more. His strength returned, but he didn't leave.

Why leave? Go where?

No, he'd stay with the fox, the fox that fed him, looked

after him and kept him warm. So he did just that, sleeping underground and eating eggs, an astonishing quantity of eggs, at peace and safe at last.

He didn't know how long he'd been with the fox. A long time, maybe no time. He knew nothing now but the fox and the eggs.

One day he woke up and the fox was gone.

He looked down at himself and saw that he was covered in fur, that he was the fox. Maybe he had always been the fox. Happy in that thought, he continued living and sleeping in the den, surviving on the eggs. Until, one day, the eggs ran out.

He looked at himself. He was no longer covered in fur. He was a bonfire Guy of jaundiced flesh and knotty gristle, glued together by sweat, snot, shit and piss. Acidic fumes rose off him, tainting the air.

Then, one night, men came. They tore the den apart and burned him out.

Fire in the hole. Time to run again.

He ran, darting into the night, avoiding human eyes, in and out of side streets and backstreets, from Highgate, back down Archway and Holloway Road, the homing instinct kicking in again, bringing him all the way back to the Angel, all the way to Myddelton Street. He was on his way, so very close to home.

Turning the corner of Chadwell Street, he saw men coming towards him. Most likely they were of no consequence, just young men, loud and drunk, on their way home. But they should not see him now, because no man could be trusted. So he leapt over the low front wall adjoining the street and ran along the side of the house to the back. The light from the ground-floor window, orange and faint, fell softly on the garden.

He scraped at the door of the shed. A shape moved inside across the ground-floor window and seconds later the back door of the house opened.

He hunched on all fours, in the shadows between the swing and the tree, staring at the man standing in the doorway, feet wide, arms folded across his hard chest, peering into the darkness.

With luck, he won't see me.

But he did see him. He spotted him easily. Because Jack's eyes missed nothing.

Night shift

Jack thought the man might attack, so he stepped back and made a fist, ready for him. He doubted, though, that this ragged, half-starved creature, crouched on all fours, could put up any sort of a fight. Still, he knew his own reflexes had been slowed.

It was after midnight. He'd smoked something very strong and was just letting it do its work when he heard the noise from the garden and decided he'd better take a look.

He had no need to punch him. The ragged man bared his teeth for a moment and then fell over on one side. Jack walked over for a closer look. He was as thin as a pin, his skin yellow everywhere it wasn't black.

Jack half-lifted, half-dragged the man into his small studio flat. He tore and cut off the rags that still clung to him, carried him to the shower, sat him on the cold floor, stood back and turned on the water. The man woke with a yelp as the first cold jets struck him, and rattled like he might break into pieces. But the hot ran in quick enough and he settled. Jack kept him there until the oily, black water had run clear, and the hot had run cold.

He dried the man as best he could. He showed no interest in doing it himself. He sat, passive on the chair, as Jack lifted and lowered his arms, moved his legs apart, then together again, and rubbed hard the long, brittle locks of hair to press out as much water as he could. He dressed him, in just underwear and an old T-shirt, wrapped him in a thick winter blanket that he kept in the wardrobe and laid him out on the only bed.

Jack poured them both a drink, set the man's on the bedside table and placed a plastic bowl on the floor in easy reach. He dragged a chair close to the bed and sat, drink in hand, waiting.

When the drink had wormed through him, the man sat up in the bed. Jack grabbed the plastic bowl and held it under his chin. He jack-knifed at the waist, lashing the bowl with vomit. He let out a long, deep sigh and lay back on the pillow.

'There now,' Jack said, feeling his pulse. 'Breathe easy. In a while, you'll be ready for another.'

A few minutes later the man's eyes rolled, gesturing towards the drink on the side.

Jack got up, lifted the glass, sat on the edge of the bed,

cupped the man's head in his other hand, and put the glass to his lips. He drank it down, a few choking drops stinging his cracked lips. He soon got the hang of it and took in a good, deep gulp.

Jack fetched a glass of water and put it to the man's lips. He grabbed at it with both hands, as if to swallow it all.

'Easy,' Jack said. 'Just rinse, then spit.'

He did as he was asked.

Jack sat back in his chair and waited, studying the man's face closely, the blue eyes turned black.

'Do you want to sleep?' Jack asked.

He shook his head and pointed to the tip of his tongue, resting on his lower lip like a piece of torn leather.

'To talk?' Jack asked.

The man nodded and mumbled something.

Jack leaned in closer to hear.

'The first,' the man said.

'The first?'

The man nodded again.

'The first what?'

'The first I knew that my next-door neighbour, Peirce, was dead was when I heard the police breaking down the door one evening, shortly after I got home from work...'

Once he'd started, Jon, as he called himself, could not stop. Jack sat with him through the night, listening patiently until Jon had told him everything – about Mark, Herman, Mercer, the studio, the trunk, Tommy, every detail – conjured in shared space, one person's thoughts the other's words, with

251

Jack leading the way. Together, they inhabited, remembered and animated it all, in sound and four familiar dimensions, and many others rolled up tight, mysterious and inscrutable. Events rearranged and condensed themselves as needed, for greater mutual understanding. This was the spirit, the fluid principle, of the drug that Jack had come to master over the course of many years.

His story done, Jon fell asleep.

Jack sat, thoughtful, in the shimmering silver morning. He checked the calendar. It was the twenty-first of March. Of course it was. He knew that already.

He fell asleep in the chair.

That evening, he had a scrub-up and a change of clothes. He left Jon wrapped in warm blankets on the bed and told him he'd be back later.

Outside, in the street, he made plenty of space in the back of the van.

The studio near Old Street was easy enough to find, the image of it still clear in his mind. The pointers were all there. He figured out the rest. It was his territory, after all.

When he arrived, the door was unlocked. He pushed it open and walked inside. He waited in the darkness for the lift to arrive, the dusty silence suddenly disturbed by industrial whirring and trundling.

Upstairs, it only took a moment to figure out that, for a party, the turnout had been very low.

At first glance, Jack thought the place completely empty. Then he saw, from the back, the top of a man's head. He was sitting silent and still in his chair, staring at an object on the floor at the far end of the room, his plump fingers resting on the arms of the chair. Even from behind, Jack could tell he was far from happy.

Jack took a few more steps into the room's dust-bowl grubbiness, its dormant irritation, bristling invisible. He knew the man had heard him, but still he didn't turn.

Jack passed the chair, casting a sideways glance at the man, confirming easily that it was Herman, who, Jack noted, registered his presence with an almost imperceptible movement of the head, his eyes still fixed on the object.

Jack walked over to it and bent down for a closer look. The trunk was open. Mark's stones had been piled inside and were covered, mainly, in a yellowish-brown substance, sometimes blackish-red. He could make out, here and there, lumps of gristle and bone, and flaps of human skin.

On top of the stones, centred in pride of place, interlaced and rotting, lay three human penises, recently thawed.

The stench pushed its fingers to the back of his throat. He focused, taking in the details, holding his breath, trying not to gag.

Above, crudely fixed to the wall, a simple title-plate bore the words: *And the Word was made Flesh*.

'So, this is it, then?' Jack asked, turning to face Herman. 'This is the work? This is the flowering of your best?'

'Yes,' Herman said. 'Made it myself.'

'All by yourself?'

Herman pouted.

'I see you managed to open it,' Jack said.

'What?'

'The trunk?'

'Mercer opened it.'

'He even did that for you.'

'Even that,' Herman said. 'Especially that.'

'Shame. Still, did many come?'

'Not many.'

'In fact, did anyone come at all?'

'In fact, no one came at all.'

'Also a shame,' Jack said. 'After all your hard work. Nicely lit, though. They got that right.'

'Yes, they got something right.'

'So, a foul inversion? Is that the idea?'

'Good, don't you think?'

'Not really,' Jack said. 'In fact, a bit obvious. Been done before, I expect.'

'Everything's been done before,' Herman said. 'I expect.'

'Why bother then?'

'I think you're missing the point.'

'I really don't think it's me who's missed the point.'

Herman shrugged. 'Do I know you?'

'I'm Jon's friend.'

'Jon? You mean Bill?'

'If you like.'

'I don't like,' Herman said. 'I don't like him at all.'

'Is that a fact?'

'In fact, it is.'

'What don't you like?'

'Weakness.'

'Ah, that.' Jack looked around. 'Mercer not here?'

'Sadly, no. He has matters to attend to. Things have been difficult lately. He's tying up loose ends and making arrangements for our return to Prague.'

'He's taking you with him?'

'Yes, we have a place—'

'Up by the Castle?'

'Yes.'

'When do you leave?'

'Tomorrow.'

'I don't think so,' Jack said. 'Will you excuse me a moment?'

'I'll excuse you for as long as you like. I have no wish to detain you at all.'

Jack went into Jon's cell, lifted his wallet from the bedside table and slipped it into his back pocket. He lifted the metal box and the moneybags off the shelf and went back out.

'Oh, I see,' Herman said. 'It's about the money. It's always about the money.'

'Not this time.'

'No?'

'No.'

'Why not?'

'Because it just isn't,' Jack said, raising the metal box high with both hands and bringing it down hard on Herman's head, smashing him to the floor in a heap. Jack brought the box down again, angling it so that one corner dug deep into the flesh and crushed the bone. The blood poured freely from the gash, down into the cup of his mouth, where it bubbled like the juice of dark summer fruits.

Jack fetched the bone-handled hunting knife from the kitchen and walked slowly back to where Herman lay, twitching and gurgling. He knelt beside him, slit his throat from ear to ear, cut out his larynx and threw it to one side.

'You don't speak,' Jack said. 'You don't speak anymore.'

Herman didn't get up again.

Jack went back to the kitchen, lifted the sweet jar off the counter and dropped it and the knife into the waxcloth bag. He carried the bag, the metal box and the moneybags downstairs and loaded them into the van. He took his time loading the rest, everything he thought of value or use. The Chinese screens and the trunk, its contents tipped onto the floor next to Herman's body, took a bit of time.

Jack went back up, took one last look, double-checking he'd left nothing of value behind. Satisfied he'd missed nothing, he got a box of matches from the kitchen, lit one and dropped it onto the pile of fat, stones and bone. The fat sizzled and the flame took quickly, licking its way up Herman's trouser leg.

Back home, Jack unloaded what he could into the garden shed. Unsure at first what to do with the trunk, he dragged it into the garden. The smaller bits and pieces, he carried to his room.

Setting some things on the bedside table, he knew immediately that Jon was not sleeping but dead. His eyes were open, his hands upraised, skin as yellow as a church candle, mouth snapped open in fixed surprise, an icicle of sugar spittle at one corner.

Jack leaned over and closed his eyes.

He sat with the body into the early hours.

He carried the body outside, still wrapped in the blanket, and put it in the trunk, the knees pressed into his chest. He placed the moneybags on him first, to cushion the brittle flesh and fragile bones. He then lowered the metal box gently into place.

He closed the lid, went back to the shed, took the spade from the hook on the wall and started digging in the patch of ground between the tree and the swing. He dug all night until the hole was deep enough. He slid the trunk in and filled in the hole. Come daybreak he was still working hard to smooth away all signs of disturbance. Despite his best efforts, a bump remained between the tree and the swing. He never did manage to flatten it.

No sooner had he buried him than he had second thoughts. It might be better to bid him farewell on a funeral pyre. The rubber tyre would get the fire going and the shed was full of junk to stoke the flames. So he dug him up again.

No sooner had he done so than he reconsidered again. The fire, the smoke, especially from the rubber tyre, would draw too much attention. So he buried the trunk again.

He was just patting down the last grains of earth as daylight broke. He sat on the ground and felt a lump in his back pocket. It was Jon's wallet. It was in better condition than his own, so he decided to keep it. He didn't think Jon would begrudge him.

He put the spade back in the shed, closed it, went to his room, tidied up a bit and threw the window open wide to let out the smell. He changed the bedding, bagging the old for burning, later. He lay down and stared at the ceiling.

I'm done with this place. Time to move on.

Sleep took its time coming, but when it did, it stayed until early evening. He got up, had a scalding shower and scrubbed up well. He had an appetite on him for life like he couldn't believe, like he'd never had before.

After a meal to line his stomach, he went to a bar, ordered a drink, a few more, and then a few more. Eventually, he noticed a woman watching him. She was with another woman, chatting away, throwing him glances, and finally she came up to the bar to order drinks, positioning herself very close. In the haze of drink, he noticed her soft, creamy hands. He could smell them, and wanted to taste them. Fresh, clean, pure, they suddenly seemed like a very good idea.

'Can I get you anything?' he asked her.

'Maybe you can,' she said, not at all coy.

So he did.

One for the road

He lay on his back on top of the hill, watching the knife describe a perfect rotation through the air. It turned handle to blade, blade to handle, frame by frame, brilliantly delineated against the stars. As he focused, it became a mandala embroidered into the depthless blue-black pelt of some infinite animal. He saw it move, kinetic star to star, its viscera pulsing, sinuous in flex and contraction. He embedded himself in its contours and breathed in.

He raised an arm and invited the bone of the handle to slip into his palm. Grasping it, he rose up into the air and hung suspended for a moment, before turning, end to end, describing his own perfect rotation against the stars. As he spun, head over heels, and round again, he saw, far below, that the stain on the ground, next to the table, had dried out in a dark, misshapen patch, like the imprint of a body fallen from a great height.

'You lived there? Myddelton Street?'

'Like I said, I moved on.' Jack's voice was all around him.

'You burned the building?'

'Gutted it.'

'And no one asked any questions?'

'People always ask questions. Doesn't mean they always get answers,' Jack said. 'And, guess what, that happens all the time. With bodies found in burned-out buildings and barbershops, and all points in between.'

'You buried the other one?'

'Laid to rest, with due care and respect.'

'In the lead trunk, between the tree and the swing?'

'I told you that spade was trying to get your attention.'

'But not,' he said, pointing down at the shop, 'in that trunk.'

'Because?'

'Damp lead? I don't think so.'

'Smart boy. Greed is great for the eyes,' Jack said. 'Let's hope it gives you strength too.'

'For what?'

'The journey home.'

'I'm not ready—'

'You're as ready as you'll ever be.'

He looked down again at the misshapen patch.

'What is that stain?' he asked.

'What stain? Oh, that stain,' Jack said. 'That's you.'

He looked down again and saw Jack sitting alone at the table. He looked to his left, to his right and all around.

He was alone, among the stars above the hill. He saw, too, in every direction, an infinite number of knives, mandalas and hills, and an infinite number of lives, suspended, each spinning through its cycle, each seeing in all directions, an infinite number spinning, and each, in turn, seeing an infinite number.

'Time gentlemen, please,' Jack said. 'Have you no homes to go to?'

He turned one more full cycle in the air. The knife slipped from his hand and shot downwards towards his tiny fenced-off world. It hit the table, bounced into the air, landed on its side and spun, its rattling tattoo abruptly silenced as Jack placed a precise finger on the thin bridge between handle and blade. Then he looked up at him and winked.

He breathed out and fell all the way.

He shot upright, hands pressed, either side, to the ground still warm from the day before. He looked around. There was no stain, no misshapen patch. He looked up at Jack, who seemed quietly pleased with himself. On the table, he saw the knife, his empty glass and the bottle, at least two-thirds full.

'How long have I been lying here?'

'Since the second drink. Two is all it takes.'

'And you've been sitting there all the time?'

'Well, every trip needs a guide,' Jack said.

'A guide?'

'To the fluid principle of the drug. A principle to which you were no stranger anyway.'

'But—'

'It really is time gentlemen, please. Kindly respect the neighbours on your way out. This is a residential area,' Jack said, clapping his hands, getting up and walking into his workshop. He returned, set a silver, moon-shaped drinking flask on the table and stood looking down at him, arms folded, feet wide apart.

'What's this?' he asked.

'One for the road. That's your lot,' Jack said, walking through the shop and unlocking the front door.

'But why bury the money with him?' he called after him.

'Because he'd earned it,' Jack said, walking back into the yard.

'I don't understand—'

'Of course you don't,' Jack said. 'But that's for you to figure out. Or not. Either way, I'm done here. Now, you know your way out, don't you?'

'I can't get up.'

Jack walked over, grabbed him under one arm and hauled him to his feet, stuffing the silver flask into his jacket pocket.

'I can't walk.'

'Then crawl.'

A look told him Jack meant it, so he sank to his knees and crawled on all fours.

'Let me give you a hand,' Jack said, seizing him by the crown of his hair, dragging him through the shop, pausing briefly to bang his head, here and there, on the trunk and other solid bits and pieces before throwing him out onto the street.

His forehead hit the kerb, cutting him above the right eye.

Jack paid no attention, said nothing, simply waited for his feet to clear the doorstep so he could pull the door hard shut and lock it.

On his knees, he covered his eyes with his hands to shelter them from the shards of morning as he looked up into Jack's face.

'You're going that way, I believe,' Jack said, pointing towards the Angel.

'Yes,' he said, 'that way.'

'Mind how you go.'

Jack turned on his heel and set off in the opposite direction.

With this ring

She saw him out with a whispered goodbye and a mutual, barely spoken promise that they would meet soon. Some time next week, maybe. He'd call. All right. She'd wait to hear from him.

She looked both ways to see if any of the neighbours were about.

No. Good. Don't they know anyway? What odds now?

The door shut with a soft click.

As it turned out, she'd never see him again.

She stopped to examine herself in the mirror by the front door. Her eyes, tired in the cool, grey morning light, took time to coax her reflection, soft, small, round and silver, into focus. She roughly fixed her hair and tugged lightly at her dressing-gown belt, tying it tight but not too tight.

That'll do.

By the time she'd reached the kitchen, the belt had already loosened. She sighed and tugged it tight around her, fussing at the frayed ends.

Time to get a new one.

She sat down with a cup of coffee at the large wooden table and ran her hand over its ancient varnished surface, grey-brown with deep black wrinkles and gouges, yet smooth everywhere to the touch. She eyed her acquisitions from yesterday, still wrapped in newspaper.

There isn't room for those plates. I must stop. The house is full to bursting already. We don't even need them. Not like we're in the habit of throwing lavish dinner parties. Or small dinner parties. Or any sort of party.

As if in response, the waxcloth bag crackled in waking on its chair, like a plastic cat, fat, old and tired. She got up, grabbed it, squeezed it into a tight ball and stuffed it deep into the bin. She'd just sat down again and raised the cup to her lips when the back door opened as softly as the front one had shut.

'You look terrible,' she said.

'I've been up all night,' Jack said.

'What's new?'

'Never much.'

'Making mischief – again?' Her words floated for a moment before settling, like powdered glass, on the table.

'Yes, again.' Jack paused. 'I suppose that's right enough.'

Not the usual tone. What's this now? Guilt, remorse or something else altogether, something only Jack would be capable of?

265

She set down her cup. The word 'kindly' seemed to fit, she concluded, grudgingly. Not that Jack's tone was ever actively unkind, not to her anyway. It was just that, generally, overt kindness was absent, or contented itself with lurking nearby in case it was ever called upon to present itself in a crisis.

Jack looked around the kitchen, making a short 'Mmm' noise to himself, as if hoping for a prompt, from the furniture, the crockery, maybe even the bin. He nodded, walked into the hall and busied himself with nothing much.

Not like himself at all. Very odd. But then, when was the last time anything and everything to do with Jack wasn't somehow odd?

She watched as he needlessly straightened a few pictures and then, not sure where to put himself, came back into the kitchen.

'I'm sorry,' he said.

'For what?'

'The life I've given you.'

She sat back in her chair, looked at him directly and enjoyed a full startled moment. 'You didn't give it to me. I took it. Don't be so presumptuous as to take the credit. Or the blame. I'll accept responsibility for my own mistakes, my own choices, thank you very much.'

'Fair enough. Still, I'm sorry all the same.'

'For what?'

'For not being who or what you thought I was.'

'I've never had much of an idea who or what you are Jack, and I stopped puzzling myself over it years ago.'

'Then I'm sorry for that too.'

'Stop saying sorry. You've said it three times in less than a minute. That's three times more than you've said it in all the years we've been married.'

'That's not true.'

'No, but it's nearly true. The spirit of it is true – and that's even worse.'

'How does that work?' He seemed genuinely curious.

'Oh, never mind. It just does.'

'Then I'm sorry for that too.'

She set her cup down hard. 'Sorry is no use, Jack. Sorry is too late. Sorry is wasted years and spent life.'

'I know,' he said, wandering out into the hall again, looking up and down, and around, at everything and, as far as she could make out, still at nothing in particular.

'Reckon this would all fetch a good price now, don't you think? A lot more than we paid for it,' he said.

'Are we thinking of selling now, is that it? Nice of you to consult me. Any specific reason?'

'I'm not,' he said.

She raised an eyebrow.

'We're not,' he said, matter-of-factly, running his fingers up and down door frames, and tapping walls and small window-panes, hidden behind plants long unused to his touch.

'I take it you're not working today.'

'No, no work today.'

'Not even later?'

'No, not even later.'

'That's not like you.'

'No,' he said. 'But it's going to be a lot like me, for a while now, from now on maybe, who knows?'

'Right, I see,' she said. 'Retirement, is it? Well, thanks for letting me know.'

'Money's not a worry,' he said with an itchy sniff, turning to look directly at her, brushing any such concern, if that's what it was, lightly but firmly aside.

'I wasn't asking about money, Jack.'

'I know that.'

She accepted this but didn't really believe it. She had long suspected that Jack had always been convinced that, at the back of everything, people were always talking or thinking about money, or things very close to money – and that pretty much covered everything people got bothered about.

'Right, well, just so long as we're clear on that,' she said. 'Well, as it's turning out to be a momentous morning – although momentous in what way exactly, I'm still not entirely sure – would you like some breakfast? We have eggs. I could make your favourite.'

'Maybe later. I'm too tired to eat.'

'Well, then, go to bed. You look wretched.'

'I'm sure I do.'

'Jack?'

'What?'

'Would you not have a bath or a shower before you go to bed?'

He peered at her through half-shut eyes. Anyone unknown

to Jack might easily, just then, have thought he'd taken grave offence and fear the conversation was about to take a turn for the worse. But she knew better.

'I'll have a wash later,' he said, in a tone that suggested he was grateful for the suggestion and would take it under advisement.

'Will you now?'

'Yes, I definitely will.'

'Fine then. I'll make sure the water's hot. Would you like me to wake you at any particular time?'

'Will you do something for me?'

'What?'

'Cancel the cards. The bank and credit cards – cancel them.'

'Why?'

'Please, will you just do this one thing?'

One thing? The cheek of him, after all these years, after all she's put up with.

'You are the strangest man,' she said, eyes fit to pop.

'Not quite,' he said, almost with a smile. 'There are stranger men out there.'

'Well, I hope I never meet them.'

'So do I.' He smiled. 'Anyway, will you do it for me?'

She hurled a look of frustration at him like a stone at an old wall. 'All right, if that's what you want.'

'Thank you.'

'And order new ones, I assume? Or have we dropped out of the banking system entirely? Is the Cronin household to become a cash economy now, is that it?'

'New ones, yes, thank you. Like I said, there's nothing to worry about.'

'You're welcome, I suppose. Will there be anything else?'

'In your name only.'

'What?'

'The cards – order them in your name only.'

'What's going on Jack? Have you pulled a bank job or something? Can I expect a firm knock at the door any moment? Front and back?'

'Is that likely?'

'How in God's name would I know what's likely, given that you just waltz in, after being out all night, and spring this on me? No discussion. No consultation. Cryptic as ever. Jesus, why am I even surprised anymore?'

'Will you just do it for me,' he said. 'Please.'

That tone again. What is all this?

'If you say so.'

'Thanks.'

'Glad to be of service. Now, will there be anything else I can do for you this increasingly momentous morning?'

'No, thank you.' He turned and walked towards his bedroom door.

'Jack,' she called after him.

'Yes?' He turned to face her.

'We should get a divorce.'

'No need.'

'Seriously.' She stood her ground.

'Seriously, no need.' He turned again and went into his

bedroom, shutting the door behind him with a click so soft that other doors might envy it, if only they could hear.

She stared at the shut door and at the plates in their wrapping, and thought of throwing them, one by one, at the wall. But she didn't. For a whole minute she stood, biting her lower lip, demanding of herself, had any other woman – anywhere, ever – married a man so infuriatingly inscrutable?

That coffee's ruined. Will I make fresh? No, I'll go up and have a nap. Sunday, day of rest, is that how we're playing it now? Has he got religion, is that it? Well, two can play at that game.

She woke in the grey-pink light, full of aches and sweet groans, stretching, twisting and wriggling, turning the pillow to find a cool patch. Through a watery crust, one half-open eye caught sight of the clock. She hadn't meant to sleep that long.

'Must get up,' she muttered.

An hour later, she did.

She washed the few dirty dishes that she herself had piled into the sink, squeezing out the dishcloth, strangling any last drops into surrender before draping it over the tap. Then she washed and dried her hands. She spent a few moments rubbing moisturising cream deep into the skin, until every sweet drop had melted to a light, reflective sheen. She opened the kitchen window and padded gently into the hallway, enjoying a slow, delicious yawn.

'Jack, are you awake?' She tapped him gently. Getting no response, she tapped more firmly. 'Jack, it's late. Do you want coffee? Something to eat maybe?'

When he still didn't respond, she opened the door, tentative at first, hopeful that the sound of the handle might be enough to wake him or draw from him some bit of an answer. When still he said nothing, she opened the door and went in. The dry, acrid air caught her by the throat.

A few minutes later, she came out, a loose fist pushed deep into the pocket of her bathrobe.

In the living room, she sat on the crimson velvet sofa, picked up the phone and dialled. The tone was strangely soothing, lulling her almost to sleep again just as someone picked up.

'Marie?'

'Yes, hello.' The voice at the other end sounded very like her.

'It's Sarah.'

'Yes, I know it is,' Marie said. 'What is it, Sarah? What's wrong?'

'It's Jack,' Sarah said, staring at the wedding ring in the cup of her hand.

'Jack? What's he done this time?'

'The last thing I expected,' Sarah said. 'He's died.'

Packed and ready

Helen, Jez and Laura were packing the last of her things into the boot when he turned the corner. They saw him coming and hurried to finish. He placed one hand on the wall to support himself, pressing the other to his forehead to stem the flow of blood.

'Laura, get in the car,' Helen said, unlocking both back doors before sliding herself onto the front passenger seat. 'Laura, get in.'

Laura clutched a small leather bag to her stomach and stared at him.

'I'm sorry,' he said, moving towards her. His legs crumpled and he fell at an awkward angle, banging his shoulder into the wall and sprawling flat on his back.

'Laura, let's go,' Jez said, climbing into the driver's seat and locking the door.

'Get in,' Helen said. 'He's not your problem anymore.'

Laura got in, slammed the door and strapped herself in as the car drove off.

The journey was silent for a good fifteen minutes as each tried to gauge the others' moods.

'Could we do with a coffee? I could do with a coffee, after all that,' Jez said, finally.

'God, yes,' Helen said. 'But will anywhere be open? It's still early. And it's Sunday. Oh, I know where.'

'Where?' Jez asked.

'You know, that little place, you know, oh God, what's it called?' Helen said, failing to remember the name, but directing Jez all the same.

'Oh, I know which one you mean,' he said.

A few minutes later, they were there. Jez turned off the ignition, unfastened his seatbelt and asked, 'Right, what do we want? My shout.'

'What would you like?' Helen asked, turning to look at Laura, squeezed among boxes and bags on the back seat.

Laura knew what they were doing – creating a moment for her to speak to Helen, to soothe the morning's ugliness. That was thoughtful of them. One of the first things she'd noticed about them was that they were always kind, if a little stiff, a little too polite about everything. But she must make a note never to forget that they were kind; not to let familiarity crumble to neglect.

'Coffee, please,' Laura said.

'What sort?' Jez asked.

'A cappuccino, please. Strong one. Double shot.'

'Double-shot cappuccino coming up,' Jez said. 'Helen?'

'The same, thanks.'

Jez got out and crossed over the road to the café. Helen waited until he was inside, then smiled at Laura. 'Everything's going to be all right.'

'You must think I'm very stupid,' Laura said.

'Why?'

'To have got involved with him in the first place.'

'No, I don't think you're stupid,' Helen said. 'I didn't know him, but I do know that people are not always what they seem.'

'He was so sweet and charming when we first met. So polite, so well spoken. Impeccable manners.'

'Handsome too. Have to give him that,' Helen said. 'Handsome men don't even have to try. Nature has already given them a leg-up.'

'Even that went.'

'I don't understand.'

'When I first met him, being with him felt like the most natural thing in the world. It felt so good. So completely right. I was...'

Helen sat quietly, dutifully listening, picking at threads on the driver's seat.

'I didn't know I could hate. But I know it now. He taught me that, and called it love. I don't care if he drinks himself to death. Or overdoses. I hope he does. It would be the right thing. He'd be no loss.'

Helen stared into the rear-view mirror.

275

'The way he is, he should…'

'And what is he like?'

'He is what he wants.'

'And what does he want?'

'To believe that he wants me. And for me to believe it too.'

'But he wanted to marry you.'

'No, he wanted me to marry him.'

'What did you say, when he asked?'

'That I needed to think about it.'

'Did you?'

'Yes. I was thinking about it,' Laura said. 'But it was so sudden, too early and probably wrong. But that's not what he expected. He expected me to say yes, immediately, no pause for thought, nothing to consider, not even the practicalities. And that wasn't good enough for him, and it was suddenly clear that what I wanted or thought didn't matter. That's when I found out what he was really like, just how much…'

'How much what?'

'Just how much he needs cruelty to feel alive.'

Helen swallowed hard, maybe trying to figure out what that meant, maybe deciding she'd rather not know.

'It all turned so cold, so quickly. Like a sickness, like the blood had been drained out of him, out of me. I couldn't bear to touch him or smell him or taste him. It was like he'd died. Or worse. He disgusted me. And the next thing I know, I'm pregnant. With a less-than-dead man's child.'

'How did…?'

'Careless. Stupid. Just…'

Helen reached back, squeezed her hand and took a moment. 'If you hadn't…?'

'What?'

'If you hadn't lost…?'

'I don't know. It was a baby. It wasn't him. There was so much else…'

'What else?'

'Things he said. Too many places, too many jobs, too many stories. He was too young. It just didn't add up. None of it.'

Helen nodded. 'Well, it's over now.'

'Is it?'

'Yes, of course it is. You'll see. You can stay with us until you've got yourself sorted. For as long as it takes.'

'Thank you,' Laura said. 'But I won't be under your feet for long, I promise you.'

'As long as it takes,' Helen said again, taking both her hands and squeezing them even tighter. 'You're still young. You've got so much ahead of you. You'll see.'

The driver's door opened and Jez climbed in, carrying three coffees in a cardboard holder. 'Everything all right?'

'Yes, everything's fine,' Helen said.

They drank their coffees and drove off. Half an hour later, they were home.

In all the time Laura stayed with Helen and Jez, the very short time it took for her to sort herself out, she wore a look that said her bag was packed and ready, and just as soon as possible, she'd be off.

She was as good as her word.

Over the fence

Laura got in, slammed the door and strapped herself in as the car drove off. He pulled himself to his feet and watched it drive steadily around the square, disappearing down the side street by the church.

Run after her? Not worth it. It was over. She was irrelevant. He had something much more important to do now.

He staggered around the corner to find the front door open. He walked down the hallway, clinging to the wall for support, and stopped at the door to his flat. He took the silver flask out of his right-hand pocket to search for his keys. Not there. He stuffed it back in and found them in his left-hand pocket.

His place was in a worse mess than he remembered. On the broken, dust-covered mirror, a torn corner of coloured card clung to the glass, hanging on by a broken nail of

Sellotape. On the floor, scattered shreds. The top drawer of the dresser was hanging out like a drunk's tongue, and the top was covered with loose change, empty wallets, bank cards and credit cards.

He ran his hand lightly over them, as if performing a ritual, summoning the dead. The lonely country lad, abused, confused and recently orphaned, befriending a stranger on the bus. His doe eyes and thick baby lips. The returning soldier, dutiful, angry and sad, senseless drunk in a bar. The medical orderly dismissed for abusing patients – the confessional boast coaxed out after several whiskies, several lines and even more lies. The warm linseed light in the rims of drinking glasses, the stains on the table, the black spark scratching ignition in his eyes.

Had an irresistible face ever met an immovable wall so hard, so bloody, so satisfying? Bone and teeth, all over the place.

Wallets. Easier to love, easier to inhabit, than flesh. No use now, any of them. Wrong money. All spent anyway.

He went out and opened the back door to the garden. There, among the shed's collapsed innards spewed out onto the grass, lay the spade, its shaft angled towards him, an invite still open, demanding his attention.

How deep? To bury a body in a trunk? Deep enough.

He picked up the spade and made a start. He kept on digging as the day warmed up and the sweat ran off him in acrid, oily streams, washing away yesterday's encrusted sweat, and that of the day before, trading new grime for old, adding fresh salt to stale.

His shirt, trousers, socks and underwear stuck to him like melted plastic. His shoes were so hot. The leather seemed to be remoulding itself, its molten black tongue licking itself into every curve and wrinkle to form a new skin he'd never peel off without tearing his own flesh.

He kept digging, driving the spade deeper into the hard earth. He tasted something like burnt rubber rising up from his hot skin. And something else, too, something metallic, like hot iron.

Fuck me, I stink.

He stopped, turned and looked at the piles of soil he'd heaped between the swing and the tree. Letting out an exhausted grunt, he spat out a dark-green clot of phlegm, raised his foot high and brought it down again with all the force left to him. And when that ran out, he borrowed some more from anger and stole the rest from hate.

The spade sliced with satisfying cut after cut through the soil, finally connecting with something – something hard by the sound of it. He dropped the spade and fell to his knees, scraping at the earth with his hands. He pulled hard, tearing an object from the ground, falling backwards onto the grass with the effort.

Sitting upright, he stared at the bent, rusted shed key in his hand, suddenly aware of Jack's wallet in his back pocket, digging into him. He reached around and pulled it out. A piece of white card, folded and torn at one corner, fell from its folds and landed on his lap. He dropped the wallet, picked up the card and unfolded it.

It was a photograph of himself and Laura, in this garden on a summer's day. The photograph he had taped to the mirror, not so long ago, when he had decided he was going to ask her – decided she was going to marry him. The photograph he had torn off in blind hungover fury the day before and slipped into his pocket on his way out. The only thing of value he could find in his room, and which he forgot all about the moment he saw William R Deal dying in the street and smelt an opportunity too good to miss. William Deal, whose wallet, snatched and slipped into the same pocket, took the torn edge of the photograph into its soft leather folds and held it there, until Jack opened the wallet and the photograph fell to the floor, to be pushed under a small side table, a detail overlooked.

He stared at it. Laura was sitting on the swing, a hint of bliss in the line of movement between her shoulders and her thighs, while he himself stood to one side, hands firmly gripping the ropes, looking every inch the loving, protective male, ready to push her, longing to catch her – playing the role as he'd observed others play it.

They were both smiling. She was so pretty but wore it like it didn't belong to her. Or feared that's what people thought. Her head inclined to one side, as if she hoped the prettiness would slip off, so she wouldn't have the burden of it anymore.

It was supposed to be different with her. She was meant to fix him. She wasn't allowed to say no.

He turned it over and read in his own handwriting: *Jon and Laura, Myddelton Street, June 2009. Happy at last.*

Jon. Which one was he? No idea. No doubt his wallet lay on the floor, among the others, his account drained, like all the rest.

Underneath, in a different hand: *You haven't earned it. Jack.*

Jack, you tricky little bastard.

He looked at the key in one hand and the photograph in the other. He set both in his lap and tugged the silver flask out of his pocket. The time had come, sooner than he thought. He uncorked the flask and took a long, harsh swig. He looked around and everything looked back, telling him he was broken, made wrong, plain and simple, and finally out of luck. And he knew it. He could not be reformed, only remade.

He took a breath, looked up and threw himself off the ledge of his mind, hoping that his rising rage would lift him again. But it didn't come. The last of it bled out of him, drawing him into the fracture.

His body knew he'd been lying there a long time. He'd been cold, very hot, and then cooler again. With half-open eyes, he could just make out the shape of a man walking slowly down the hill towards the fence. The man reached the fence, stopped and rested one arm on it.

'Morning,' the man said.

'Is it morning?' he asked.

'It is.'

'Already?'

'Yes.'

'Again?'

'It comes around so quickly.'

'Doesn't it just,' he said. 'You've been here before, haven't you?'

'So have you.'

'I should get up.'

'You should.'

'I will, later.'

'You been busy today?'

'Yes, I have.'

'Digging for gold?'

'Something like that.'

'Find any?'

'Not today,' he said. 'Found this though.' He searched blindly for the key, found it by his side and waved it in the air.

'Any use?' the man asked.

'No,' he said. 'No use.'

'Why not?'

'No lock.' He laughed and nearly cried.

'I see you've had your poison,' the man said, pointing to the empty moon-shaped flask.

'Saw me coming,' he said, summoning what strength he had left to pick up the flask and throw it at the shed, only for it to ricochet back and land on his chest.

'Always.'

'I could have turned back.'

'Spilt milk.' The man sighed, turned and started to walk back up the hill.

'Maybe this time,' he called after him, holding up the key and then dropping it.

'Maybe,' the man called back, without turning. 'Your choice.'

'You'll be back?'

'Let's hope not.'

The man disappeared over the brow of the hill.

Something hopped onto his face. Something green. Maybe a frog, maybe not a frog. It hopped off again, and away. He sensed it sitting in the grass, looking at him.

He crawled into the hole and placed the photograph and key on his chest. He swept as much of the loose soil over him as he could, lay back, drained the last drops in the flask, closed his eyes and sank into the hole, loosening himself to leach through the skin of the world, into the formless cathedral. Remembering everything, forgetting everything, with nothing to stop him and no one to catch him, he gathered himself again, remembering forgotten, forgetting forgotten, and everything still to do.

Aeroplane

He was late, the new owner. Only a little, but late all the same. Could something have gone wrong, even at this stage? No, of course not. Her solicitor had confirmed that the money was on its way to the bank.

Stop worrying, for God's sake.

Sarah winced at the deep drag marks on the floor.

That old trunk, I expect. Hope they've been noticed before now. I can't be doing with any last-minute arguments over the cost of new floors or re-polishing or whatever.

Last night, she dreamt about the place.

Everything is bundled together – huge, old, broken and ugly, tied up in a net, resting, impossibly balanced, on the rickety wooden trolley high up on a cliff top, on a fresh, breezy day, a touch of powder blue behind the tumbling silver white. Her step quickens as the trolley rolls towards the edge.

So much change in so short a time. Policemen and doctors, family and funeral, one brisk bit of business after another.

True to his word, Jack did have a wash later. At the hands of an undertaker. But that was Jack for you. He did have a very annoying habit of being right, though rarely in ways you could expect or predict.

She smiled at Dr Fisher as he walked back into the kitchen.

'Well, that's the first time he's ever been an easy patient,' Dr Fisher said.

'I can imagine,' Sarah said. 'Still, I know he was fond of you.'

Dr Fisher looked genuinely surprised.

'So, the heart…' Sarah said, neither question nor statement.

'Yes, indeed, the heart. But, to tell you the truth, the rest wasn't far behind.'

'The rest?' Sarah asked, noting that Dr Fisher warmly offered complete hopelessness by way of small comfort.

'You know…' Dr Fisher indicated vaguely, with a circling finger, at the general area of the abdomen. 'The principal internal organs. Altogether too much…'

'I see. Well…'

'I'll leave you to get on. They'll be here shortly, to…'

'Yes, of course. Good, yes.'

'Will you be all right? Can I…?'

'No, I'm grand. My sister Marie is here.'

'Ah, of course.'

She saw him out with a smile she would practise often, without perfecting, in the coming weeks.

She didn't smile at the policeman. It didn't seem appropriate. Besides, he was young. She felt no need to smile at young men. They seemed pleased enough with themselves these days. Didn't need her encouragement.

'Why, Mrs Cronin, do you think your husband misled the bank and the police about how he came to be in possession of Mr Deal's wallet?' the bright and shiny policeman asked.

Sarah told him only what she knew, and no more, just as Jack had asked her to do the day he died. Because there, in his clean, spartan room, on his bedside table, next to his wedding ring and the folder containing all the papers relating to his financial affairs, lay William R Deal's wallet on a sheet of paper with the instructions: *Ring the police. Tell them who you are. This wallet was stolen from a dying man, by the young man asking about the trunk. I redeemed it on behalf of the deceased. Don't try to hide anything and don't worry. The rest will follow. Jack.*

'It wasn't always possible to understand why Jack did half the things he did,' Sarah said. 'And on this occasion, I can only guess that he did it to protect himself.'

'From?'

'From that young man. Whatever his name was.'

'So, your husband thought he was dangerous? Why do you say that?'

'Just a guess. Perhaps he rumbled him.'

'What makes you think that?'

'Jack had a nose for people. He knew them and what they were about. I never knew anyone to hoodwink Jack.'

'After you left, what happened exactly?'

'Between Jack and the young man?'

'Yes.'

'I honestly have no idea.'

'He said nothing about it when he came back?'

'Not a word.'

'And you don't find that strange?'

'Relative to what?'

He looked puzzled. 'Mrs Cronin, you're sure your husband didn't know him?'

'As sure as I can be.'

'What does that mean?'

'Are you married?'

'No.'

'Thought not.'

He looked even more puzzled, perhaps a little annoyed. 'What did your husband tell you when he came back?'

'Very little.'

'Did he do anything out of the ordinary?'

'Well, he died,' Sarah said. 'Even by Jack's standards, that was out of the ordinary.'

'Before he died, Mrs Cronin.'

'He told me to cancel our bank and credit cards and order new ones in my name only.'

'Why?'

Her turn to be annoyed. 'Because, obviously, that young

288

man had stolen his and he knew he was going to die.'

'How did he know that?'

'It's my husband we're talking about. He just bloody would.'

'I see.'

'I'm glad you do,' Sarah said.

The policeman bit his lip.

'The man who died, who was he?' Sarah asked.

'He was training to be an actor. Not long in London. Recently down from the North.'

'I see. That's very sad.'

The policeman nodded.

'And the other young man? The thief?'

'What about him?'

'Any sign, any word?'

'No trace. Just a ransacked room, a big hole in the garden, a trashed shed, a headless teddy on the swing, a bent shed key and an angry landlord. Basically, he's in the wind.'

'Maybe he belongs there. Maybe you should leave him there.'

'Don't worry. One day, the wind will drop and he'll fall right into our lap.'

Sarah took the hard glimmer in his eye as a hint that they should leave it at that. Fine by her. She'd had enough of this business, which, the way she saw it, was none of her business.

And that, as far as the police were concerned, was the end of the matter as regards Mrs Sarah Cronin. She was free to go. So she did. Straight to the funeral director.

He smiled at her. She couldn't decide whether that was appropriate or not.

The funeral was brisk, mercifully short on cant or sentiment. Family, in as much as Jack could be said to have had family, turned up dutifully. As for the rest – best described, in the main, as associates not friends – they were respectful but ever conscious of the time.

A restaurant meal was laid on, because the etiquette of dying demanded it. Nothing too fancy or pricey, of course. Jack wouldn't have approved.

'Why do people feel a need to eat when they're seeing off the dead?' he once asked her. 'Nothing kills my appetite like a corpse.'

It was an oddly stiff and sober occasion, too, and Jack wouldn't have approved of that. Still, it was brisk, that was the main thing. He'd have given the nod to that all right, Sarah thought, from behind his half-shut eyes, making that low hum in his throat.

She smiled at the thought.

Yes, the hum. It at least told you that he was thinking, where words generally failed to tell you what he was thinking.

Over a slow glass of red wine, Sarah looked around and caught Marie's eye with a look that said *Who the hell are these people?*

Who the hell was Jack? Marie's look shot back, without missing a beat. An answer of sorts. And not a bad one, truth be told.

A few stragglers turned up, at various points, generally late, and certainly all after the funeral itself. Marie raised an eyebrow to Sarah at the sight of one or two of them and whispered, 'Freeloaders, don't you think?'

'No, they look odd enough to have been friends of Jack's.'

One of them came over to pay his respects to Sarah, sincerely enough she felt. She asked how he knew Jack.

'Oh, Jack and I were refugees together, going back a long way.'

'Refugees? From what war?'

'From the one that never ends,' he said, with a sage nod and a distant look that suggested if he didn't have another drink very soon, or something stronger, this could prove to be a long and difficult day.

'Definitely one of Jack's,' Marie muttered out of the corner of her mouth.

All hands shaken, all condolences expressed and thanks given, Sarah, Marie and her husband were the last to drop with heavy relief onto the back seat of a taxi.

'Tell me,' Sarah asked, 'at what point did funerals become like awards ceremonies?'

'About the same time as christenings and weddings and the rest,' Marie said. 'What did you think of the food?'

'Pretentious and too much of it.'

'A bit of that, I suppose, right enough.'

'Remind me not to eat there when I die.'

They burst into giggles, stifled in the instant the driver tensed in his seat and threw a look at the rear-view mirror.

'You'll come back to ours?' Marie asked.

'For a while,' Sarah said. 'But I must get back.'

'Stay the night. Stay one night Sarah. Stay two. Stay as long as you like.'

'I have things to do.'

'What things?'

'Sell the shop,' Sarah said. 'And everything in it. Every last bowl and stick.'

Every last bowl, stick and trunk.

She winced again at the scratch marks on the floor.

That's a deep gouge there and no mistake. Oh well, the ink's on the paper, the money's in the bank. Just about. Caveat emptor.

Still no sign of the new owner.

Why didn't she just leave the keys with the estate agent? Why had she put herself in the position of even having to be here? Some phantom of sentiment second-guessing her even as she insisted, to herself and anyone willing to listen, that she wanted nothing more now than to be done with this place for good?

The impatient tap of her foot courted a small, sharp echo. The place looked much more spacious with all the stock gone, sold quickly and cheaply to sweeten the deal and hasten the sale for the new owner, so that he could get on, without delay, with his bold new entrepreneurial reinvention.

When they first met, he felt a need – perhaps courtesy, maybe self-regard, she couldn't tell and didn't care – to detain her with the details. A cool flash of her eyes seemed to tell him that she had little call to know and even less to pretend that she did.

Yes, he was late and, just as she was telling herself that this would be the last time she'd wait for any man, or waste life wondering what he was up to or who he was with, the new owner arrived, bright with apologies, mumbling about traffic and roadworks. She airily waved it all away. He was here, at last. That was all that mattered.

The exchange complete, they shook hands.

'Well...' he said.

'Well, best of luck with it all.'

'Thank you. And to you.'

She offered a thin wafer of a smile, left without a backward glance and was almost at the corner in the tinkling of the bell.

As she approached the Angel, she stuck out her hand and hailed a black cab.

'Highgate,' she said, strapping herself in.

Marie was already at the spot, alone, settled on the warm grass, a picnic cloth spread out, a hamper waiting.

'Are they not coming?' Sarah asked, no attempt to conceal her disappointment.

'Yes, they'll be here in a bit,' Marie said. 'Doctor's appointment. I mentioned it.'

'Oh yes, of course you did. Sorry.'

For a minute, the two sisters busied themselves to an unnecessary degree, unpacking food, drink and paper napkins, laying out paper plates and plastic forks and cups, and tearing and puffing at fiddly plastic packaging. That milked for all it was worth, they had no choice but to sit quietly and meet each other's look.

'God, it's been a hectic few weeks,' Sarah said.

'Hasn't it just? I'm parched. Tea?'

'I'd love one.'

Marie reached for a flask and poured them both a cup.

'I'm glad of that,' Sarah said.

'Me too.'

They sipped in silence.

'Why did you marry him?' Marie asked suddenly.

'Why does anyone marry?'

'But why marry so late? And why him? You knew very little about him.'

'Sometimes that's a good thing.'

'Is it?' Marie was shocked.

'I've always thought that if you want to like someone, you're probably better off not getting to know them.'

'Why?'

'Because people are always disappointing.'

'You mean men are.'

'Actually, I don't,' Sarah said. 'I mean people. And I include myself.'

'Did you tell him that?'

'I did. More than once.'

'And what did he say?'

'Not much. As per. I think it wasn't what he'd hoped for,

maybe. Though, saying that, not sure hope is a word I'd much associate with Jack. Any more than despair or a whole lot of other words that just had no meaning for Jack. Besides, he was nobody's fool. Took no prisoners, did Jack, and he did make me laugh. Especially in the early days.'

'When you used to come here?'

'God, yes, we came here a lot. He scrubbed up well in those days.'

'Cheap date, if you ask me.'

'Marie, say what you like about Jack – and God knows I have – but he was never mean with me. I was always well provided for. And, well not to sound showy, I'm even better provided for now. There were no flies on Jack. Just ask his accountant.'

'You worked too.'

'I didn't say I didn't. All I'm saying is that Jack never expected me to go without, and God knows he didn't spend much on himself. There wasn't much in his wardrobe to ship off to the charity shops. The needy and shoeless needn't be looking to the corpse of Jack Cronin for a good winter coat or sturdy footwear, I can tell you.'

'Fair enough.' Marie laughed, pausing only briefly before asking, 'Did you never wonder, though, what he got up to all those years he was abroad, before you met? Where it now?'

Sarah stiffened a little. Not this again. One of the many threads in the life of Jack Cronin, left hanging loose and untidy, that her sister had forever to pick at until – what?

295

– somehow she'd tidied it, found a shelf for it, brushed it into the dustpan, dumped it in a skip?

'All over the place,' Sarah said. 'He was very quiet about all that. He took a lot of drugs, I know that much. Well, you know, experimented, as they used to say.'

Marie was silent.

There, having heard what you wanted to hear, you've decided you didn't want to hear it after all.

'Did you love him?'

'I thought I did. For a bit.'

'That's a "no", then.'

'It's not "no", Marie,' Sarah said. 'It's just what I said. Your problem is, you always think everyone should think, feel and behave like you do, and if they don't, they're wrong somehow.'

'So that really is "no" then?'

'Love belongs to others,' Sarah said, her impatience chafing the seam of civility. 'And, to be honest, they're welcome to it.'

'Everyone deserves love.'

'Maybe so, but that doesn't mean everyone gets it.'

'Will you miss him?'

'Oddly, yes, I will,' Sarah said, surprising herself.

'With Jack gone,' Marie asked, dropping her voice, 'will you and he, what's he called—?'

'Eddie.'

'Eddie, yes, will you and Eddie, you know, make a go of it?'

'A go of what?'

'For God's sake, Sarah, you know what I'm getting—'

'Some sort of life together? Is that it?'

'Yes, some sort of life, yes. Why not?'

'God, no. I've given that my worst shot. Someone else can have a go. No, the minute I knew Jack was dead, I knew I didn't want Eddie either.'

'Why?'

'I haven't analysed it and I don't intend to.'

'And what did Eddie want?'

'Precisely what I didn't, if I'm honest.'

'Well, that was hard on him, I suppose.'

'No supposing about it. But life can be hard, Marie.'

'People can, you mean.'

Sarah coughed to prevent herself saying what she felt like saying, and for a moment neither said anything. Sarah stared into middle distance, and noticed a fox peek out from behind a tree. Marie squeezed her unused napkin into a ball.

'Did Jack know about Eddie?' Marie broke the silence.

'I'm sure he did, though we never talked about it.'

'Never? You two were a strange couple.'

'All couples are strange. It's a strange word. Just keep saying it over and over to yourself. You'll soon hear how strange it is.'

'That's true of any word. We played that game as children. Do you remember?'

'True enough, we did.' Sarah laughed, emptied her cup and set it upside-down on the cloth. 'And, oh, speak of the devil.'

Marie turned, saw them and smiled.

'Here's my darling boy.' Sarah held out her arms as Tommy ran towards them, arms outstretched, Mark trailing a few feet behind.

'How was the doctor's?' Marie asked as Mark kissed her and sat down.

'Fine, maybe a little bit of an ear infection, nothing serious.'

'Did he give you anything?'

'Ointment,' Mark said, reaching for a sandwich. 'How are you Sarah? All done and dusted?'

'I'm fine Mark. Yes, all done and dusted. Finally.'

'Did you pick up the ointment yet?' Marie's turn to be impatient, for no obvious reason.

'It's in the car,' Mark said, finishing his sandwich and reaching for another. 'So what now Sarah?'

'Well, I must make some calls,' she said. 'No time to waste.'

'Who do you need to call?' Marie sounded genuinely offended not to be in the know already.

'The estate agent.'

'About the shop? Isn't it all sorted?'

'No, Marie, about the house.'

'The house?'

'Yes, the house,' Sarah said. 'I'm going to sell it too, and everything in it. Every last bowl and stick.'

'Where will you go?' Mark asked.

'Somewhere new. Somewhere empty.'

Marie looked puzzled, suspicious that there was something

in this that she should worry about, if only she could pin it down. Having thought hard for a moment, she said, 'You can stay with us until you've found somewhere.'

'Can I indeed?' Sarah gave Mark a knowing look. 'There's something for you to look forward to Mark.'

'He won't mind,' Marie said. 'Will you?'

'Of course not,' Mark said. 'Stay as long as you like.'

'And Tommy won't mind, will you Tommy? You'd like Aunt Sarah to come and live with us for a while, wouldn't you?'

'For ever?' Tommy, who had been running about, came to a sudden stop.

Sarah smiled at him. 'No darling, not for ever. For a little while.'

Tommy looked disappointed.

'Oh, come here and give your Aunt Sarah a big cuddle.'

Tommy fell into her with delight.

'I'll pay you rent,' Sarah said, folding Tommy into her arms.

'You've no need.'

'I've every need.'

'We have money, Sarah. Tell her we have money, Mark.'

Mark nodded, muttering something compliant, indifferent, something that said he was easy about the whole thing, through a mouthful of sandwich.

'Now you can have more. Bank it. Put it towards Tommy's education.'

'Right enough…' Mark said.

'Mark!'

'What?'

'That's settled then,' Sarah said. 'Anyway, it won't be for long. A few weeks at most. I've seen a place I like.' She stifled a yawn. 'God, excuse me, but I'm tired.'

'Here,' Marie said, taking off her light blue cardigan and making a pillow of it.

'Thank you. But you mustn't let me sleep too long.'

'We won't, will we Mark?'

'We will, yes,' Mark said. 'I mean we won't. Scout's honour.'

Sarah rested her head on the makeshift pillow, closed her eyes and turned her face to the sun as Tommy burrowed into her side, his little arms reaching to surround her.

'Tommy,' Sarah asked, 'what are you going to be when you grow up?'

'A farmer,' Tommy said, jiggling from the middle.

'It was a fireman last week,' Marie said. 'God knows what it'll be next week. Astronaut, probably.'

'I'll buy you a tractor,' Sarah said. 'Would you like that?'

'Yes.' Tommy kicked his feet in the air.

'Or maybe a pig? A big pink pig.'

'A pig.' Tommy kicked his feet even higher.

'A pig it is then.' Sarah closed her eyes and squeezed him tight. 'With a dirty big snout. Honk, honk.'

'Honk, honk.'

She squeezed him and he burst into giggles, like a tiny summer fruit popping its juice.

'Dirty big snout…'

She pressed her face deeper into her makeshift pillow, falling, tumbling on the pink and yellow marbling of the sun inside her eyelids, slipping into sleep like butter off a hot knife.

Tommy turned and lay the other way on her stomach. She rested one hand on his head, a finger lightly tracing the milky skin behind his ear, as the thin whistle of his breath rose to touch her face, fall away and rise again.

The trolley reaches the edge of the cliff. It stops, waiting for her. She reaches it. It falls off. She looks down as it crashes into the rocks and bounces, the net still intact, into the sea. It sinks to the bottom and hits a rock, loosening the net, scattering its contents and drowning waste. From beneath the rock, two fish dart free. They chase each other's tails, entwining, spiralling upwards faster and faster, finally breaking the surface, separating for ever in spume of silver and gold.

Sarah opened her eyes. Something old, knotted and deep escaped her in a breath. She slept again until Marie tapped her shoulder. And when she woke, she felt better.

Through half-shut eyes she saw Tommy a few feet away, running round and round, soaring in widening circles, making engine noises, with his arms out to his sides, full stretch at shoulder height.

Because Tommy was his own aeroplane.

Shutting up shop

The new owner shut the front door behind Sarah and walked out back into the small, off-square yard. Looking around, he wondered whether the space could be put to much practical use. His hand drifted onto the battered metal table and, for a few minutes, he stood there, lips pursed, eyes clicking in beady calculation, fingers absently tapping the well-worn surface as it sucked in the heat of the day.

The workshop door banged in the breeze. As he went to shut it, he noticed the broken handle.

Someone should have seen to that before now. No matter.

He stepped inside.

The air hung like a scorched tapestry, its tarred threads still giving off fumes. As his eyes adjusted, he could make out idle benches and tools, shelves stacked with glinting bottles and coloured jars, full and half-full of cloudy and clear liquids, and odd pieces of laboratory equipment – metal pipes, flasks, angle-brackets, a Bunsen burner and the like. The nauseating smell of gas, spent flame and combusted chemicals, barely masking the gag-making tang of rodent piss, shot up his nostrils and down his throat, instantly triggering a headache.

Poking around he found, in one corner, cardboard boxes crammed full of papers and books, dusty covers and dustier subjects, among piles of crime magazines. The faded black and green cover of one magazine showed a man with a broad toothbrush moustache, smiling – a sharp glint in his eyes, almost certainly for very wrong reasons. He flicked through the pages with an expression suggesting he should disapprove but was privately intrigued. He rolled it up and stuffed it, as best he could, into his jacket pocket.

Something wedged down the side of one box caught his eye. He reached in and pulled out a roll of paper, flattened and badly creased. It was a chemistry degree, brittle and yellow, ink and ribbon faded, unwilling to be unfurled after all this time. He let go of one torn end and it snapped back into its long sleep. He shoved it back in, turned, lifted a bottle at random off a shelf, opened it and sniffed the contents with a mixture of curiosity, suspicion and disgust. He set it back on the shelf.

He made more rough calculations.

Any of this lot worth anything at all? Some, maybe, but it's mostly junk. Not worth the time. Pile it into a skip and have done with it.

He stepped back into the light, sucked down fresh air and eyed up the workshop itself.

Tear it down. You can make better use of the space. And it's the only way you'll ever get rid of that terrible smell. How did anyone ever work in that?

That settled, he dragged the battered metal table across the ground, tipped it up on one side, prised the legs from their catch, folded the table flat and propped it against the door, wedging it tight beneath the broken handle.

There now. That, in the meantime, will keep the smell in and the rats out.

He went back into the shop and locked the back door behind him. He flipped the sign on the front door to 'Closed' and stepped outside, locking it and double-checking it was secure. As he walked away, he could just hear the last tinkle of the bell.

Out back, the sun struck the underside of the table, lighting a series of odd markings, accidental maybe, or an equation perhaps, a formula of some kind – the means, finally, to coax something of lasting value out of hiding. Or maybe, just remnants of the secret language of children at play, one long and brilliant summer's day, scratched with stone in the metal, and then forgotten.

46529877R00168

Made in the USA
Charleston, SC
21 September 2015